FM

D1355765

UNCOVERING
THE
SILVERI SECRET

UNCOVERING THE SILVERI SECRET

BY

MELANIE MILBURNE

First published in Great Britain 2013
by Mills & Boon, an imprint of Harlequin (UK) Limited.
Large Print edition 2013
Harlequin (UK) Limited, Eton House,
18-24 Paradise Road, Richmond, Surrey TW9 1SR

© Melanie Milburne 2013

ISBN: 978 0 263 23192 2

Harlequin (UK) policy is to use papers that are natural, renewable and recyclable products and made from wood grown in sustainable forests. The logging and manufacturing process conform to the legal environmental regulations of the country of origin.

Printed and bound in Great Britain
by CPI Antony Rowe, Chippenham, Wiltshire

To my niece Bethany Luke—an absolute sweetheart who cares about everybody. XOX

CHAPTER ONE

IT WAS the first time Bella had been home since the funeral. Haverton Manor in February was like a winter wonderland, with a recent fall of snow clinging to the limbs of the ancient beech and elm trees that fringed the long driveway leading to the Georgian mansion. The rolling fields and woods beyond were shrouded in a thin blanket of white, and the lake shone like a sheet of glass in the distance as she brought her sports car to a stop in front of the formal knot garden. Fergus, her late father's Irish wolf-hound, gingerly rose from his resting place in the sun and came over to greet her with a slow wag of his tail.

'Hiya, Fergs,' Bella said and gave his ears a

gentle scratch. 'What are you doing out here all by yourself? Where's Edoardo?'

'I'm here.'

Bella swung round at the sound of that deep, rich, velvet-smooth voice, her heart giving a funny little jump in her chest as her eyes took in Edoardo Silveri's tall figure standing there. She hadn't seen him face-to-face for a couple of years, but he was just as arresting as ever. Not handsome in a classical sense; he had too many irregular features for that. His nose was slightly crooked from a fist fight, and one of his dark eyebrows had a scar through it, like a jagged pathway cut through a hedge, both hoofmarks of his troubled adolescence.

He was wearing sturdy work-boots, faded blue denim jeans and a thick black sweater that was pushed up to his elbows, showcasing his strong, muscular arms. His wavy, soot-black hair was brushed off his face, and dark stubble peppered his lean jaw, giving him an intensely masculine look that for some reason always made the back of her knees tingle. She took in a little jerky breath and met his startling blue-green eyes, almost putting her neck out to do it. 'Hard at work?' she said, adopting the aristocrat-to-servant tone she customarily used with him.

'Always.'

Bella couldn't quite stop her gaze drifting to his mouth. It was hard and tightly set, the deep grooves either side of it indicating it was more used to containing emotion than showing it. She had once come too close to those sensually sculptured lips. Only the once, but it was a memory she had desperately tried to erase ever since. But even now she could still recall the head-spinning taste of him: salt, mint and hot-blooded male. She had been kissed lots of times, too many times to recall each one, but she could recall Edoardo's in intimate, spine-tingling detail.

Was he remembering it too, how their mouths had slammed together in a scorching kiss that had left both of them breathless? How their tongues had snaked around each other and duelled and danced with earthy, brazen intent?

Bella tore her eyes away and glanced at the damp dirt on his hands from where he had been pulling at some weeds in one of the garden beds. 'What happened to the gardener?' she asked.

'He broke his arm a couple of weeks ago,' he said. 'I told you about it when I emailed you the share-update information.'

She frowned. 'Did you? I didn't see it. Are you sure you sent it to me?'

The right side of his top lip came up in a mocking tilt, the closest he ever got to a smile. 'Yes, Bella, I'm sure,' he said. 'Perhaps you missed it in amongst all the messages from your latest lover. Who is it this week? The guy with the failing restaurant, or is it still the banker's son?'

'It's neither,' she said with a lift of her chin. 'His name is Julian Bellamy and he's studying to be a minister.'

'Of politics?'

She gave him an imperious look. 'Of religion.'

He threw back his head and laughed. It wasn't quite the reaction Bella had been expecting. It annoyed her that he found her news so amusing. She wasn't used to him showing any emotion, much less amusement. He rarely smiled, apart from those mocking tilts of his mouth, and she couldn't remember the last time she had heard him laugh out loud. She found his reaction over the top and completely unnecessary. How dared he mock the man she had decided she was going to marry? Julian was everything Edoardo was not. He was sophisticated and cultured; he was polite and considerate; he saw the good in people, not the bad.

And he loved her, rather than hating her, as Edoardo did.

'What's so funny?' she asked with an irritated frown.

He swiped at his eyes with the back of his

hand, still chuckling. 'I can't quite see it some-how,' he said.

She sent him a narrowed glare. 'See what?'

'You handing around tea and scones at Bible study,' he said. 'You don't fit the mould of a preacher's wife.'

'What's that supposed to mean?' she asked.

His eyes ran over her long black boots and designer skirt and jacket, before taking a lei-surely tour of the upthrusts of her breasts, fi-nally meeting her gaze with an insolent glint in his. 'Your skirts are too high and your mor-als too low.'

Bella wanted to thump him. She clenched her hands into fists to stop herself from actually doing it. She wasn't going to touch him if she could help it. Her body had a habit of doing things it shouldn't do when it came too close to his. Her nails bit into her palms as she tried to rein in her temper. 'You're a fine one to talk about morals,' she threw back. 'At least I don't have a criminal record.'

Something hardened in his gaze as it pinned hers: diamond-hard. Anger-hard. Hatred-hard. 'You want to play dirty with me, princess?' he asked.

This time Bella felt that tingly sensation at the base of her spine. She knew it had been a low blow to refer to his delinquent past, but Edoardo always triggered something dark, primal and uncontrollable in her. She didn't know what was it about him that got her back up so quickly, but he needled her like no other person.

He had *always* done it.

He seemed to take particular delight in getting a rise out of her. It didn't matter how much she promised herself she would keep a lid on her temper. It didn't matter how cool and sophisticated she planned to be. He *always* got under her skin.

Ever since that night when she was sixteen, she had done her best to avoid her father's bad-boy protégé. For months, if not years, at a time she would keep her distance, barely even acknowledging him when she came home for a brief visit to her father. Edoardo brought out something in her that was deeply unsettling. In his company she didn't feel poised and in control.

She felt edgy and restless.

She thought things she should not be thinking. Like how sensual the curve of his mouth was, the way the lower lip was fuller than the top one; how his lean jaw always seemed to need a shave. How his hair looked like it had just been combed with his fingers. How he would look naked, all tanned, whipcord-lean and fit.

Like how he always looked at her with that hooded, inscrutable gaze as if he was seeing through the layers of her designer clothes to her tingling body beneath...

'Why are you here?' he asked.

Bella gave him a defiant look. 'Are you going to march me off the premises for trespassing?'

A glint of something menacing lurked in his gaze. 'This is no longer your home.'

Her look hardened to a cutting glare. 'Yes, well, you certainly made sure of that, didn't you?'

'I had nothing to do with your father's decision to bequeath me Haverton Manor,' he said. 'I can only presume he thought you were never very interested in the place. You hardly ever visited him, especially towards the end.'

Bella's resentment boiled inside her—resentment and guilt. She hated him for reminding her of how she had stayed away when her father had needed her the most. The permanency of death had made her run for cover. The thought of being left all alone in the world had been terrifying. The desertion of her mother just before her sixth birthday had made her deeply insecure; people she loved *always* left her. She had buried her head in the social scene of London rather than face reality. She had made the excuse of studying for her final exams, but the truth was she had never really known how to reach out to her father.

Godfrey had come to fatherhood late in life, and after her mother had left, he had not coped well with the role of being a single parent. Consequently their relationship had never been close, which had made her insanely jealous of the way in which her father had fostered his relationship with Edoardo. She suspected Godfrey saw Edoardo as a surrogate son—the son he had secretly longed for. It made her feel inadequate, a feeling that was only reinforced a hundredfold when she found out the way her father had left his estate. 'I'm sure you worked my absence to your advantage,' she said, shooting him another embittered glare. 'I bet you sucked up to him every chance you could, all the while painting me as a silly little socialite with no sense of responsibility.'

'Your father didn't need me to point out how irresponsible you are,' he said with that annoying, trademark lip-curl. 'You do a fine job of that all by yourself. Your peccadilloes are splashed across the newspapers just about every week.'

Bella simmered with fury even though there was some truth in what he said. The press always targeted her, making her out to be a wild child with more money than sense. She only had to be in the wrong place at the wrong time for some ridiculous story to come out about her.

But things would be different soon.

Once she was married to Julian, the press would hopefully leave her alone. Her reputation would be spotless. 'I'd like to stay for a few days,' she said. 'I hope that won't inconvenience you?'

Those intriguing eyes glinted dangerously again. 'Are you asking me or telling me?'

Bella put on a beseeching expression, her hatred of him tightening her spine until she could feel every knob of her vertebrae. It was positively galling to have to ask for permission to stay at her childhood home. That was one of the reasons she had turned up unannounced. She'd figured he might not be able to turn her away with the household staff looking on. 'Please, Edoardo, may I stay for a few days?' she asked. 'I won't get in your way. I promise.'

'Do the press know where you are?' he asked.

'No one knows where I am,' she said. 'I don't want anyone to find me. That's why I came here. No one would ever dream of finding me here with you.'

His chiselled jaw was locked like a vice, a muscle on the left side moving in and out like a tiny heart beating under the skin. 'I've a good mind to send you on your way.'

Bella pushed her bottom lip out. 'It's about to snow again,' she said. 'What if I run off the road or something? My death would be on your hands.'

'You can't just turn up here and expect the red carpet to be rolled out for you,' he said with a look of stern disapproval. 'You could at least have called and asked if it was all right to stay. Why didn't you?'

'Because you would have said no,' Bella said. 'What's the problem with me staying a few days? I won't get in your way.'

The muscle tapped a little harder in his jaw. 'I don't want a bunch of voyeurs lurking about the place,' he said. 'As soon as the paparazzi turn up, you can pack your bags and leave. Got it?'

'Got it,' Bella said, inwardly seething at his overbearing manner. What did he think she was going to do—call a press conference? She wanted to escape all that and lie low until Julian came back. She didn't want any more scandals in her life.

'And nor will I tolerate you bringing friends here to party all hours of the day and night,' he said, drilling her with his diamond-hard gaze. 'Understood?'

Bella gave him her best 'I'll be good' face. 'No parties.'

'I mean it, Bella,' he said. 'I'm working on a big project just now. I don't want to be distracted.'

'All right, already. I get it,' she said, flashing an irritated gaze. 'So what's the big important project? Is she female? Is she currently sleeping over? I wouldn't want to cramp your style or anything.'

'I'm not going to discuss my private life with you,' he said. 'Before I know it, you'd be spilling all to the press.'

Bella wondered who his latest lover was, but there was no way she was going to ask. Asking would imply she was interested. She didn't want him thinking she spent any time at all musing over what he was doing and whom he was doing it with. He mostly kept his private life exactly that—private. His enigmatic, unknowable nature made him a target for the paparazzi but somehow he managed to keep his head below the parapet. Whereas Bella couldn't seem to step outside her house in Chelsea without attracting a camera flash from the lurking paparazzi, who always painted her as a professional party girl with nothing better to do than get a spray tan.

Her engagement to Julian Bellamy would hopefully put all that to rest. She wanted a clean slate, and once she was married, she would have it. Julian was the nicest man she had ever met. He was nothing like the men she had dated in the past. He didn't attract scandal or intrigue. He didn't party or drink. He didn't have a worldly bone in his body. He wasn't interested in wealth and status, only helping others.

'Would you bring in my bags for me?' she asked Edoardo with mock sweetness. 'They're in the boot.'

Edoardo leaned against the front fender of her car, one ankle crossed over the other, his arms folded against the broad expanse of his chest. 'When do I get to meet your new lover?' he asked.

Bella pushed her chin a little higher. 'He's technically not my lover,' she said. 'We're waiting until we get married.'

He laughed again. 'Holy mother of Jesus.'

She threw him a look. 'Do you mind not blaspheming?'

He pushed himself away from her car and came to stand close enough for her to smell the heat of his arrantly male flesh: sweat and hard work with a grace note of citrus that swirled around her nostrils, making them involuntarily flare. She took a prickly little breath and stepped backwards but one of her heels snagged on the crushed limestone and she would have fallen but for one of his hands snaking out and capturing her by the wrist.

Her breath completely halted as his long, tanned fingers gripped her like a steel manacle. An electric charge surged through her skin as soon as those calloused fingers made contact with her skin. She felt it sizzling all the way to the bones of her wrist; they felt like they were going to disintegrate to fine powder. She swept her tongue out over her lips as she tried to muster as much icy hauteur as she could, but even so her heart fluttered like a hummingbird behind the scaffold of her ribs as his eyes meshed with hers. 'What in God's name do you think you're doing?' she asked.

One corner of his mouth came up in a sardonic smile. 'Now look who's blaspheming.'

Bella's stomach dropped like an out-of-control elevator when his thumb pressed against her leaping pulse on the underside of her wrist. She hadn't been so close to him in years. Not since *that* kiss. Ever since that night, she had assiduously avoided any physical contact with him. But now her skin on her wrist felt like it was being scorched. It felt hot and tingly, as if electrodes had zapped the nerves. 'Get your filthy hands off me,' she said but her voice came out raspy and uneven.

His fingers tightened for an infinitesimal moment, his unusual blue-green eyes holding hers, sending a riot of sensations tumbling down the length of her spine. She could sense *him* so close to her pelvis, that essential part of him that defined him as a virile and potent male. Her body felt its primal magnetic pull just as it had all those years ago. What would it feel like to press against him now that she was no longer that gauche, inexperienced, slightly inebriated teenager?

'Say please,' he said.

She gritted her teeth. *'Please.'*

He released her and she rubbed at her wrist, shooting him a livid glare. 'You've made me all dirty, you bastard,' she said.

'It's good clean dirt,' he said. 'The kind that washes off.'

Bella looked at the cuff of her shirt below the sleeve of her jacket that now had a full set of his dusty fingerprints on it. She could still feel the pressure of his fingers as if he had indelibly branded her flesh. 'This shirt cost me five-hundred pounds,' she said. 'And now you've completely ruined it.'

'You're a fool, paying that for a shirt,' he said. 'The colour doesn't even suit you.'

She stiffened her shoulders in outrage. 'Since when did you become a personal stylist?' she jeered. 'You don't know the first thing about fashion.'

'I know what suits a woman and what doesn't.'

She scoffed. 'I bet you do,' she said. 'The less clothes the better, right?'

His eyes glinted as they did a lazy sweep of her form. 'I couldn't have put it better myself.'

Bella felt her skin tingle all over as if he had physically removed her clothes, button by button, zip by zip, piece by piece. She couldn't stop herself from imagining how his work-roughened hands would feel on the softer smooth skin of her body. Would they catch and snare like a thorn on silk? Would they scratch or would they caress? Would they…?

She pulled back from her wayward thoughts with a hard mental slap. 'I'm going inside to say hello to Mrs Baker,' she said and swished past him to go to the front door.

'Mrs Baker is away on leave.'

Bella stopped as if she had suddenly come up against an invisible wall. She turned around to look at him with a quizzical frown. 'So who's doing the cooking and cleaning?' she asked.

'I'm taking care of it.'

Her frown deepened. 'You?'

'You have a problem with that?' he asked.

Bella blew out a little breath. She had a very *big* problem with it. Without Mrs Baker bustling about the place, she would be alone in the house with Edoardo. She hadn't planned on being alone with him. It was a very big house, but still…

In the past he had lived in the gamekeeper's cottage. But, since her father had left him Haverton Manor, he had the perfect right to live inside the house. He managed her father's investments and operated his own property-development business out of the study next to the library. Apart from the occasional business trip abroad, he lived and worked here.

He slept here.

In *her* house.

'I hope you don't expect me to take over the kitchen,' Bella said, shooting him another glare. 'I came to have a break.'

'Your whole life is one long holiday,' he said with a sneer that boiled her blood. 'You wouldn't know how to do a decent day's work if you tried.'

Bella gave her head a little toss. She wasn't going to tell him about her plans to help Julian fund his mission work with a good chunk of her inheritance. Edoardo could jolly well go on thinking she was a flaky airhead just like everybody else. 'Why would I need to work?' she asked. 'I have millions of pounds waiting for me to collect when I'm twenty-five.'

The muscle near his tightly set mouth started hammering again and his eyes turned to blue-green granite. 'Do you ever spare a thought for how hard your father had to work to make his money?' he asked. 'Or do you just spend it as fast as it's dropped in your account?'

Bella gave him another defiant look. 'It's my money to spend how I damn well like,' she said. 'You're just jealous because you came from nothing. You got lucky with my father. If it hadn't been for him, you'd be pacing a prison cell somewhere, not playing lord of the manor.'

His eyes glittered with sparks of acrimony. 'You're just like your gold-digging bitch of a mother,' he said. 'I suppose you know she was here a couple of days ago?'

Bella tried to disguise her surprise. *And hurt.* She hadn't seen or heard from her mother in months. The last time she had heard from Claudia was when she'd called to say she was moving to Spain with a new husband—her second since her divorce from Bella's father. Claudia had needed money for the honeymoon. But then, Claudia always needed money, and Bella always felt pressured into giving it. 'What did she want?' she asked.

'What do you think she wanted?' he asked, that hard gaze glittering with cynicism.

Bella gave him an arch look. 'Maybe she wanted to check you were still managing my assets properly.'

A frown suddenly pulled at his brow. 'If you want a blow-by-blow inspection of the books, then all you have to do is ask,' he said. 'I've offered to meet with you more regularly but you've always refused. The last three meetings, you didn't even have the decency to show up in person.'

Bella felt a little ashamed of herself. She had no question over his management of her father's estate. The profits had steadily grown from the moment he had taken over the share portfolio in the months before her father had died from cancer. His street-smart intelligence and clever intuition had saved her assets where other investors' had been lost during the economic turmoil of the past few years.

A couple of times a year he would insist they meet so he could go through the estate books with her. At first she had suffered those meetings, all the while sitting silently seething at how he was in control of her life. But even in that large, swanky London office he had seemed a little too close to her. The last meeting she had attended in person, her mind had wandered off into dangerous territory as she sat staring at the dark pepper of stubble around his mouth as he patiently explained the stocks and shares. She had tried to focus but within seconds she had started gazing at his hands as he had turned the pages of the meticulous report he had prepared. He had looked up at one point and locked gazes with her. She still remembered the throb of that silence. She had felt it deep inside her body.

She could still feel it.

'That won't be necessary,' Bella said. 'I'm sure you're doing all you can to keep things in order.'

There was a tight little silence.

'Are you expecting your boyfriend to join you?' he asked.

Bella tucked a strand of hair back behind her

ear that the chilly breeze had worked loose. 'He's away on a mission in Bangladesh,' she said. 'I thought I'd come here until he gets back.'

'London nightlife losing its appeal?' he asked.

She gave him a brittle glare. 'I haven't been to a nightclub in ages. It's not my scene any more.'

'Prayer meetings more your thing?'

Oh, how she hated him for his mockery. 'I bet you've never got down on your knees in your life,' she tossed back.

His eyes slid to her pelvis and back with deliberate slowness. They seemed to burn with a secret erotic message as they met hers. 'Say the word, princess, and I'll be on my knees before you can say "heavens above."'

Bella's insides coiled and flexed with hot, traitorous desire. It simmered between her thighs. A flickering pulse that made her aware of every muscle and nerve and cell at the feminine heart of her.

He was the bad boy from the wrong side of

the tracks. She was the rich heiress with a pedigree that went back centuries.

She was about to become engaged.

It was forbidden.

He was forbidden.

Bella gave him a frosty look. 'I don't think there's a prayer on this earth that could save your soul,' she said.

'Why not try some laying on of hands instead?' he said with a bitter smile.

She felt that disturbing little flicker again. It made her hate him all the more. She hated that he could have this effect on her, even now. How could he make her body act so shamelessly wanton just by being near him? It annoyed her that he had so much sensual power over her. It shocked her that she couldn't control her reaction to him. It was even more shocking to know he was well aware of his impact on her. She could see it in those darkly brooding, indolent looks he gave her. The slow burn of his gaze made her skin feel like it was going to melt off her bones. 'Go to hell,' she bit out through tightly clenched teeth.

'You think I haven't already been there?' he asked.

Bella couldn't hold his gaze. It seemed to burn through her like a laser beam, touching her, stroking her, making her feel sensations she should not be feeling.

She turned on her heels and marched inside, closing the door with a satisfying clunk of metal and wood.

Edoardo let out a long hiss from between his teeth once she had gone inside the manor. He clenched and unclenched his fist a couple of times but he could still feel the tingling of where his hand had touched her wrist.

He should have frogmarched her back to her car and sent her packing. She was nothing but trouble.

And temptation.

He blew out another harsh breath. Yes, well, Bella Haverton was nothing if not tempting.

She was a pint-sized little she-devil with an uppity attitude that stuck in his craw like a twig. He wanted her as much as he hated her. For years he had burned with lust for her. She was the temptation he had taught himself to resist, all except for that one night when she had pushed and pushed until he had snapped. He had kissed her roughly, angrily. The searing heat of that kiss had been building up for months and months. All those 'come and get me' looks she had been casting him, all those flirty little accidental touches as she had moved past him in the doorway had slowly but surely corroded his iron self-control. It had been like a massive explosion once their mouths met.

He still didn't know quite how he'd had the strength of will to pull back from her, but somehow he had. She had been only sixteen, young, passionate and way out of her depth. He was nine years older than her, but he was centuries older in terms of experience. He hadn't wanted to betray the trust Godfrey Haverton had placed in him. It had never been spoken in so many words, but he had always sensed Godfrey trusted him not to do the wrong thing by his young daughter.

It was different now she was older. There was no reason why he couldn't indulge in a hot little affair with her. She might fancy herself in love with some other man, but she couldn't hide the fact she still wanted him. He saw it in her eyes: the hunger, the wildfire passion she tried so desperately to hide from him.

He could *still* taste her.

All those years had passed, but he could still remember her hot, wet sweetness, the way her mouth had felt, the way it had moved against his. His body jammed with lust at the mere thought of driving into her, feeling her softness against his hardness, her arms tightly around him, her mouth on his, her tongue tangling with his in a sensual duel.

He had not touched her again until today. It had been like touching a live wire. His fingers still fizzed with the sensation. The ache to touch her again was like a pulse in his blood. It roared and screamed through his veins.

He *wanted* her.

He *lusted* after her.

There was a part of him that didn't *want* to want her. She was the one person who could make him lose control, and control was everything to him. He was not proud of the way he had grabbed her that night all those years ago. He had acted on impulse, not reason. She had that power over him.

She *still* had that power over him.

Bella always liked to play the haughty aristocrat with him. She looked down her nose at him as if he had just crawled out from a primeval swamp with his knuckles dragging along the ground. He could think of nothing better than taking her down a peg or two.

And she had played right into his hands by turning up unannounced.

He gave an inward smile. She might think she

could flounce in and take charge, issuing orders as if he was nothing but a lowly servant paid to wait on her hand and foot. Had she forgotten how her father's will was written?

He was in charge now.

And he was not going to let her forget it.

CHAPTER TWO

As soon as Bella stepped inside the foyer, she felt a pang of emptiness that was like a hollow ache inside her chest. There was no hint of pipe tobacco. No sound of a walking stick tapping against the floorboards. No sound of classical music playing softly in the background.

There wasn't even the sound of Mrs Baker singing tonelessly in the kitchen. No homely sounds of pots and pans clattering. No delicious smells of home baking, just the sharp tang of fresh paint lingering in the air and a silence that was measured by the methodical ticking of the grandfather clock: Tick, tock. Tick, tock.

She wandered through the lower floor of the manor, noting the newly painted kitchen and conservatory. The formal sitting room, overlooking the garden, the lake and the rolling fields beyond, had also had a bit of a makeover. Edoardo had spent much of the past five years restoring the manor to its former glory. He did most of the work himself. It wasn't that he was short of money; he could easily have afforded to outsource to contractors but he seemed to enjoy doing hands-on work.

Bella had only been seven years old when he had come to live at Haverton Manor. It had been the year after her mother had left. Her father had taken Edoardo on as a project, presumably to distract himself from his own misery at being deserted by his young wife and left to care for a small child on his own.

Edoardo had been kicked out of every foster home in the county. At sixteen he had clocked up enough minor offences to put him in juvenile detention until he turned eighteen. Bella remembered a surly adolescent with a bad attitude. He had seemed to wear a perpetual scowl. He solved conflicts with his fists. He swore like a trooper. He didn't have manners. He didn't have friends, only enemies.

But somehow her father had seen behind the bad-boy façade to the young man with the potential to go places and achieve great things. And under Godfrey Haverton's steady and patient tutelage, Edoardo had managed to finish school and earn a place at university, where he studied commerce and business.

Edoardo had used the leg-up to good purpose. Godfrey had given him a small loan, and from that he had purchased his first property and subdivided it. He reinvested the profits in more property, which he subsequently restored and resold. His business had grown from those humble beginnings to what was now a highly successful property-investment portfolio that was constantly expanding. He also managed her father's estate, which was held in trust for Bella until she reached the age of twenty-five. With just one year to go until she could access her substantial inheritance, Edoardo was a thorn in her side she tried to avoid as much as possible.

Each month he dutifully transferred her allowance into her bank account. She had mostly kept within her budget, but now and again an extra expense would come in and she would have to suffer the indignity of contacting him to ask him to provide her with more funds. It infuriated her that her father had set things up in such a way, that he had chosen Edoardo as her trustee rather than appoint someone else— someone more impartial. Her father had trusted Edoardo more than he trusted her, and that hurt. It made the ill feelings she had always harboured against Edoardo all the more intense. To add insult to injury, her father had given him *her* ancestral home. She loved Haverton Manor. It was where she had spent the happiest days of her life before her mother had left. Now it was Edoardo's and there was not a thing she could do about it.

Bella hated him with a passion that seemed

to become more and more fervent as each year passed. It simmered and boiled inside her. She could not imagine it ever abating.

He was her enemy and she couldn't wait until he was no longer in control of her life.

Bella moved through the upper floors, taking in the view from each window, reacquainting herself with the memories of the grand old house where she had spent her early childhood before she'd gone away to boarding school. Her nursery was on the top floor, along with a nanny's flat and a toy room that was as big as some children's bedrooms. The nursery hadn't been renovated as yet. She was surprised to find some of her childhood things were still there. She hadn't been back to pack them up since her father's funeral. She wondered why Edoardo hadn't packed them up and posted them off to her.

Going into that room was like stepping back in time to a period when her life had been a lot less complicated. She picked up her old teddy bear with his faded blue waistcoat. She held him to her face and breathed in the smell of childhood innocence. She had been so happy before her mother had left. Her life had seemed so perfect. But then, she had been very young and not tuned in to the undercurrents of her parents' marriage.

Looking back with the wisdom of hindsight, Bella could see her mother was a flighty and moody woman who was soon bored by country life. Claudia craved attention and excitement. Marrying a very rich man who was twenty-five years older than her had probably been enormously exciting at first, but in time she'd come to resent how her social-butterfly wings had been clipped.

And yet, while Bella could understand the frustration and loneliness her mother had felt in her sterile marriage, she still could not understand why Claudia had left *her* behind. Hadn't she loved her at all? Had her new boyfriend been more important than the child she had given birth to?

The hurt Bella felt still niggled at her. She had papered it over with various coping mechanisms but now and again it would resurface. She could still remember the devastation she had felt when her mother had driven away with her new lover. She had stood there on the front steps, not sure what was happening. Why was Mummy leaving without saying goodbye? Where was she going? When would she be back? Would she *ever* be back?

Bella sighed and looked out of the window. Her eye caught a movement in the garden below, and she put the teddy bear back on the shelf and moved across to the window.

Edoardo was walking down to the lake; Fergus was following faithfully a few paces behind. Every now and again he would stop and wait for the elderly dog to catch up. He would stoop down and give Fergus's ears or frail shoulders a little rub before moving forward again.

His care and concern for the dog didn't fit with Bella's impression of him as an aloof lone-agent who shied away from attachment. He had never shown any affection for anyone or anything before. He hadn't appeared to grieve the loss of her father, but then, she hadn't been around to notice all that much. He had been marble-faced at the funeral. He had barely uttered a word to her, or to anyone. At the reading of the will he had seemed unsurprised by the way her father had left things, which seemed to suggest he had a part in their planning.

She had flayed him with her sharp tongue that day. The air had rung with her vitriol. She had ranted and fumed and screamed at him. She had even come close to slapping him. But he had not moved a muscle on his face. He had looked down at her with that slightly condescending look of his and listened to her blistering tirade as if she'd been a spoilt, wilful child having a tantrum.

Bella moved away from the window with a

frustrated sigh. She didn't know how to handle Edoardo. She had *never* known. In the past she had tried to dismiss him as one of the servants, someone she had to tolerate but not like, or even interact with unless absolutely necessary. But she had always found his presence disturbing. He did things to her just by looking at her. He made her feel things she had no right to feel. Was he doing it deliberately? Was he winding her up just to show he had the upper hand until she turned twenty-five?

He had always viewed her as the spoilt princess, the shallow socialite who spent money like it was going out of fashion. When she was younger she had tried her best to understand him. She had sensed the world he had come from was wildly different from hers from the occasional snippet of gossip from the locals, but when she had asked him about his childhood, he would cut her off with a curt command to mind her own business. What annoyed her more was that he must have spoken to her father about her probing him, as Godfrey had expressly forbidden her ever to speak to Edoardo about his childhood. He'd insisted that Edoardo deserved a chance to put his delinquent past behind him. It had driven another wedge between Bella and her father, making her feel more and more isolated and shut out.

Over the years her empathy towards Edoardo had turned to dislike and then to hatred. During her adolescence she had brazenly taunted him with saucy come-hither looks in an effort to get some sort of rise out of him. His aloofness had made her angry. She'd been used to boys noticing her, dancing around her, telling her how beautiful she was.

He had done none of that.

It was as if he didn't see her as anything but an annoying child. But then, that night in the library when she'd been sixteen, she had overstepped the mark. With a bit of Dutch courage on board—compliments of some cherry brandy she had found—she had been determined to get him to notice her. She had perched on his desk with her skirt ruched up and with the first four buttons of her top undone, showing more than a glimpse of the cleavage that had begun to blossom a couple of summers before.

He had come in and stopped short when he'd seen her draped like a burlesque dancer on his desk. He had barked at her in his usual growly way to get out of his hair. But, instead of scampering off like a dismissed child, she had slithered off the desk, come over to him and tiptoed her fingertips over his chest. Even then he had resisted her. He had stood as still as stone, but she had felt empowered by the way his eyes had darkened and the way he had drawn in a sharp breath as her loose hair brushed against his arm. She'd pressed closer, breathing in the scent of him, allowing him to breathe in hers.

She could still remember the exact moment he'd snapped. He'd seemed to teeter on the edge of control for long, pulsing seconds. But then he had finally grabbed her roughly—she had thought in order to push her away—and slammed his mouth down on hers. It was a kiss of hunger and frustration, of anger and lust, of forbidden longings. It had shaken her to the very core of her being. And, when he'd finally wrenched his mouth off hers and thrust her from him, she could tell it had done exactly the same to him…

Bella pushed back from her thoughts of the past. It was her future she had to think about now.

A future that could not happen without Edoardo's co-operation.

Edoardo was in the kitchen a few hours later preparing a meal. He knew the exact moment Bella entered the room even though his back was turned away from the door. It wasn't the sound of her footfall or even the fact that Fergus opened one eye and lifted one faded steel-grey ear. It was the way the back of his neck tingled, as if she had trailed her slim, elegant white fingers through his hair. His body had always felt her presence like a sophisticated radar tracking a target. He had spent years of his life suppressing his reaction to her. He had hardly even noticed her until she had reached adolescence. But then, as if a switch had been turned on in his body, he had noticed everything: her long, glossy brown hair and those big, Bambi toffee-brown eyes with their dark fringe of impossibly long lashes.

He had noticed the graceful way she moved, like a ballerina across a dance floor or a swan gliding across the surface of a lake. He had noticed her porcelain skin, the way it was milky-white compared to his deep olive-brown. He had noticed her smell, that gorgeous mix of honeysuckle and orange blossom with a hint of vanilla. At just five-foot-five she was petite up against his six-foot-three frame. He towered over her. One of his hands could swallow both of hers whole. His body would crush hers if he took possession of her.

He *ached* to take possession of her. His body had been humming with it ever since he had grabbed her wrist outside. His fingers could still feel where they had come in contact with her skin. Her skin had felt like satin. He wondered if the rest of her body would be as silky-smooth.

How long before he caved in to the temptation? He had always been wary around her, distant to the point of rude. It wasn't just because of his sense of obligation to her father: he had a feeling she would do more than move him physically. He didn't want her to use him like she used the other men in her life. The men she dated were just playthings she picked up and put down again when her interest waned. He would allow no one—not even Bella Haverton—to use him for sport or entertainment.

'Dinner will be ready in half an hour,' he said.

'Would you like some help?' she asked.

Edoardo flicked the tea towel over his shoulder as he turned to face her. She looked young, fresh and innocent, yet worldly and defiant at the same time. It was a potent mix she had always played to her advantage. She was like a chameleon: a woman-child, a sexy siren and a doe-eyed innocent all wrapped in a knockout package.

Her clothes draped her model-slim figure like an evening glove on a slender arm. She could make a bin liner look like a million-dollar designer outfit. Her make-up was subtle and yet brought out the toffee-brown of her eyes and the lush thickness of her lashes. The lip-gloss she was wearing made her bee-stung lips all the more tempting and alluring.

She was playing her ice-maiden game now but Edoardo could see straight through it. She couldn't hide the way her body reacted to him. She was aware of him in the same way he was aware of her. There was a sexual energy in the air between them—a current, a force, that crackled every time their eyes met.

'You can pour a glass of wine for us both,' he

said. 'There's a red open over there, or there's white, if you prefer, in the fridge.'

She poured a glass of red for them both and handed him one. He felt the zap of her fingers as they briefly met his around the stem of the glass. He saw the flare of reaction in her brown eyes. *'Salut,'* he said, holding her gaze as the blood thundered in his loins.

She gave her glossy lips a quick darting sweep with the tip of her tongue. *'Salut,'* she said and lifted the glass to her mouth. It always amazed him how sensual she was, seemingly without even trying. How could taking a sip of wine suddenly be so sexy? He couldn't stop staring at her mouth, how it glistened from the wine. How her lips were so plump and full, just ripe for kissing.

'So how did you meet this boyfriend of yours?' Edoardo asked as he dragged his gaze away from her mouth.

'He was serving meals to the homeless when I walked past from the tube station,' she said.

'I thought it was amazing that he was standing out there in the cold and wet, handing out food parcels and blankets. We got talking and then we exchanged numbers. The rest, as they say, is history.'

'How serious are you about him?'

'I'm very serious,' she said, setting her chin at a defiant height. 'I want to get married in June.'

He took a measured sip of his wine and then placed the glass back down on the counter. Bella married? *Not on his watch.* 'You realise you can't marry anyone without my permission?' he said.

She blinked. 'What?'

'It's clearly stated in your father's will,' he said. 'I have to approve your choice of husband if you choose to marry before the age of twenty-five.'

Her eyes widened and then narrowed. 'You're lying,' she said. 'It does *not* say that. You're in control of my money, not my love life.'

'Go check it out with the lawyer,' he said, turning back to his chicken dish on the stove.

Edoardo could feel her anger building in the silence. It made the air heavy, loaded with anticipation, like that tense period after lightning flashed, just before the thunder bellowed.

'You put my father up to this, didn't you?' she said. 'You cooked up this little scheme to get absolute and total control of me.'

Edoardo put the wooden spoon down on the spoon holder and turned back round, folding his arms across his chest and crossing one ankle over the other. 'So why do you want to marry this Julian guy?' he asked.

She put up her chin. 'I'm in love with him.'

He laughed and unfolded his arms. 'Now, that's funny.'

She sent him a gimlet glare. 'I suppose it is to someone who doesn't have an emotional bone in his body,' she said. 'You wouldn't recognise love if it came up and bit you on the face.'

Edoardo looked at her mouth again, at those

lips he had fantasised about for years, remembering how soft and yielding they had been beneath the pressure of his. He had fantasised about them moving over his body, kissing and sucking on him until he exploded. A red-hot dart of lust shot him in the loins. He could just imagine her taking him to heaven with that sexy little mouth of hers. It would certainly make a change from her spitting at him like an angry little cat. 'Ah, yes, but I recognise lust when I see it,' he said. 'And you are positively simmering with it.'

She hissed in a little breath, her eyes flashing in fury. 'How dare you?'

'Oh, I dare,' he said, trailing a light fingertip down the length of her arm.

She pulled back from him as if he had scorched her. 'Don't touch me.'

'I like touching you,' he said in a low, growly tone. 'It does things to me. Wicked things. *Sinful* things.'

Her slim throat moved up and down agitatedly. 'Stop this,' she said. 'Stop this right now.'

'Stop what?' he asked. 'Stop looking at you? Stop imagining how it would feel to thrust inside you right to the hilt? To have you bucking and screaming underneath my—'

She raised her hand so quickly he almost didn't block it in time. He captured it within a hair's breadth of his cheek, his fingers clamping around her wrist with bruising force. 'I can do rough if you want, princess,' he said. 'I can do it any way you want it.'

'I do not want you,' she said, spitting the words out like bullets.

He felt her thighs bump against his. He felt the softness of her breasts where they brushed against his chest. He felt the drum beat of her pulse against his fingers. He felt his need race through his blood with an almighty primal roar.

It would be so easy to slam his mouth down on hers like he had done before. To taste her, to tempt her with the pleasure he could feel building like a dam inside him. She would go off like a firecracker. He knew they would be dynamite together. She needed someone strong enough to control her wild impulses and reckless behaviour. The men she dated danced around her like moths around a bright light.

He would have her. He knew it in his bones. He would have his fill of her, purging her from his system once and for all.

And she would enjoy every pulse-racing second of it.

Edoardo slowly released her wrist. 'Got that nasty little temper of yours under control?' he asked.

She gave him a fulminating look as she rubbed at her wrist. 'I pity the women you take to bed,' she said. 'They probably leave it bruised from head to foot.'

'They leave it panting for more,' he said with a smouldering smile.

She made a scornful sound. 'Why? Because you don't know how to properly satisfy a woman?'

His eyes mated with hers. 'Why don't you try me and see?'

She gave him a withering look. 'I'm about to become engaged, remember?'

'So you say,' he said. 'Has he asked you, or are you just clearing it with me in case he does?'

She gave him a reaction that reminded him of a bantam hen ruffling its feathers. 'The man doesn't always have to do the proposing,' she said. 'What's wrong with a woman asking a man?'

'That could work every four years, but this year isn't a leap year, so you've either got to buck the trend or wait.' Edoardo picked up her left hand. 'So where's the ring?'

She snatched her hand away. 'I'm having one designed specially.'

'Who's paying for it?'

She frowned at him. 'What sort of question is that?'

'So *you're* paying,' he said with a mocking look.

'I don't have to discuss this with you,' she said. 'It's none of your damn business.'

'Yeah, well, that's where you're wrong, Bella,' he said. 'It *is* my business to see that you don't get ripped off by some gold-digging sleazebag. That's why your father appointed me as your financial guardian. He didn't want you to be taken advantage of until you were old enough to understand how the world works.'

'I'm twenty-four years old!' she said. 'Of course I know how the world works. My father was old-fashioned. He was two generations older than my friends' fathers. You had no right to agree to this stupid scheme. You should've talked him out of it. I should've been given control when I turned twenty-one.'

'You were too young at twenty-one,' he said. 'I think you're still too young even now. You don't know what you want.'

Her hands were in tight little fists by her sides. 'I know I don't want you messing up my life,' she said. 'I love Julian. I want to be his wife. I want a family with him. You can't stop me marrying him. I'll fight you every step of the way.'

'Fight me,' he said. 'I'll look forward to it. But you won't win this, Bella. I will not allow your father's life's work to be frittered away by your impulsive choice of a partner. I'll put a hold on your allowance. I'll freeze your assets. You won't have a penny to buy a cup of coffee, much less pay for a wedding.'

'You can't do this!'

'How long have you known this man?'

Her cheeks blushed like a rose. 'Long enough to know he's my soulmate.'

He nailed her with his gaze. 'How long?'

'Three months,' she mumbled.

'What the—?'

'Don't say it.' She cut him off before he could let out his forceful expletive. 'It was love at first sight.'

'That's a load of crap,' he said. 'You haven't even slept with this guy. How do you know if you're compatible?'

'I don't expect you to understand,' she said. 'You don't even have a soul.'

Edoardo was inclined to agree with her. His childhood had bludgeoned his heart until he had hidden it away for ever. He had taught himself not to feel anything but the most basic of feelings. He hadn't loved anyone since he was five years old. He wasn't sure he *could* love any more. It was a language he had forgotten, along with most of his native tongue. He had taught himself not to need people. Needing people left you vulnerable, and the one thing he would never allow himself to be again was vulnerable.

'Let's leave me out of this,' he said. 'What I'm concerned about is you. You're doing exactly what your father was afraid you would do—you're letting your heart rule your head. It should be the other way around.'

'You can't choose who you fall in love with,' she said. 'It just…happens.'

'You're not in love with him,' he said. 'You're

in love with the idea of marriage and family, of security and respectability.'

She flounced to the other side of the kitchen, taking her wine with her. 'I'm not going to talk about this any more,' she said. 'I'm marrying Julian, and you can't stop me.'

'Will he wait a whole year for you?' Edoardo asked.

She lowered her glass and sent him a furious scowl. 'You heartless, controlling bastard.'

'Sticks and stones,' he said, picking up his own wine and raising it in a toast.

She slammed her glass down so hard the stem broke and wine swirled in a red arc like a splash of blood. She yelped and jumped backwards, clutching her right hand.

'Are you all right?' he asked, stepping towards her.

'I'm fine.' She bit down on her lip.

He took her hand and unpeeled her fingers to find a little gash in the pad of her thumb. 'You silly little fool,' he said. 'You could've severed a tendon.'

'It's nothing.' She tried to pull her hand away but he didn't let go. She glared up at him. 'Do you mind?'

'You need a plaster on that,' he said. 'There's a first-aid kit in the downstairs bathroom. Come with me.'

She looked as if she was going to defy him but then she gave a frustrated sigh and allowed him to lead her to the bathroom next to the conservatory. 'I can sort it out myself,' she grumbled. 'I'm not a little child.'

'So stop acting like one.'

She flashed him a furious scowl. 'Why don't you stop acting like an overbearing ogre?'

'Sit on the bath stool,' Edoardo instructed as he pulled out the drawer where the first-aid kit was stored.

She sat and held out her hand with a recalcitrant look on her face. 'It's just a scratch.'

'It's just shy of needing a stitch,' he said as he checked the wound for traces of glass.

'Ouch!'

'Sorry,' he said.

She glowered at him. 'I bet you're not.'

'You know me so well.'

She gave him a lengthy look. 'Does anyone know you, Edoardo?' she asked.

He shifted his gaze to her thumb as he carefully placed a plaster over the wound. She had switched from spitting cat to gentle dove within a heartbeat. He had seen her work her lethal charm on others. He had seen grown men fall over like ninepins when she gave them that misty, doe-eyed look. She knew the feminine power she had and exploited it whenever she could.

But he was *not* going to let her manipulate him.

'What makes you ask that?' he asked casually.

'You don't seem to have a lot of friends,' she

said. 'You don't seem to need people like other people do.'

'I have what I need in terms of companionship,' he said.

'Who is your best friend?'

He released her hand and moved to the basin to wash his hands. 'You should take care of that thumb,' he said. 'You don't want to get it infected.'

'Edoardo?'

He dried his hands on the nearest towel and then shoved it back on the rail. 'I'd better go clean up that glass before Fergus steps on it,' he said.

She bit her lip again. 'I'm sorry…'

He gave her a brief glance before he shouldered open the door. 'We all have our limits, Bella.'

CHAPTER THREE

WHEN Bella came back from the bathroom, there was no sign of the spill of red wine or any shards of glass. Fergus was still lying on his padded bed near the cooker. Edoardo was dishing up a delicious-looking chicken and tomato dish that smelt absolutely divine.

'Do you want to eat in here or the dining room?' he asked without looking up from what he was doing.

'Here's fine,' she said. 'Fergus looks like he's settled in for the night.'

'He's getting on,' he said as he set a plate in front of her. 'He's slowed down a lot just lately.'

'How old is he now?' Bella asked, screwing up her forehead as she tried to remember. 'Seven?'

'Eight,' he said. 'Your father bought him when you decided you weren't coming home for Christmas that year.'

Bella frowned when she thought of how she had behaved back then by choosing her social life over her father. It wasn't just an attempt on her part to avoid Edoardo after that kiss. Her relationship with her father had never really been the same after her mother had left. He had thrown himself into work, spending long hours in the study or going on business trips and leaving her with babysitters.

When he was at home he'd hardly seemed aware she was there. She had felt frustrated that she couldn't get close to him. She had been frightened he might leave her too and had perversely done everything she could to drive him away. She had blamed him for her mother leaving and had acted out dreadfully. She had thrown terrible tantrums. She had screamed, railed and deliberately made things difficult for him. The various nannies he had employed hadn't stayed long. In the end she had agreed to go to boarding school even though she hadn't really wanted to go. 'Was he lonely, do you think?' she asked. 'Did he miss me?'

'Of course he did,' he said, frowning slightly.

'He never said.'

'It wasn't his way,' he said.

Bella toyed with the edge of her plate. 'After my mother left…it was difficult to get close to him,' she said. 'He seemed to shut himself away. Work became his entire focus. I didn't think he cared what happened to me. I think I reminded him too much of Mum.'

'He was hurt,' he said. 'Your mother's affair totally gutted him.'

Guilt felt like a yoke around her shoulders. She had made it so much worse. Why had she been so selfish? Why couldn't she have comforted her father instead of pushing him away? She had ended up hurting him just as much as her mother. She looked at Edoardo again. 'You really cared about him, didn't you?' she asked.

'He had his faults,' he said. 'But basically he was a good man. I had a lot of respect for him.'

'I think he saw you as the son he never had,' she said. 'I was jealous about that. I never felt good enough.'

He frowned again. 'He loved you more than life itself.'

Bella gave a shrug. 'I was just a girl,' she said. 'He was of the generation where sons were everything to a man. He loved me, but I always knew that deep down he thought I was just like my mother. I suspect that's why he orchestrated things the way he did. He didn't think I had the sense to make my own decisions.'

'He was concerned you would be too trusting,' he said. 'He didn't want you to be hoodwinked by shallow charm or empty compliments.'

'So he appointed you as gatekeeper,' Bella said with more than a little hint of wryness. 'A man who never wastes time on charm or compliments.'

He took a contemplative sip of his wine. 'I can be charming when I need to be.'

She gave a little laugh. 'I'd like to see that.'

There was a little silence.

'You look stunningly beautiful tonight,' he said.

She shifted restively in her seat. 'Stop it, Edoardo.'

'I sometimes fantasise about you being in bed with me.'

She blushed to the roots of her hair. 'You're not being charming,' she said. 'You're being lewd.'

He leaned forward with his forearms resting on the table, his eyes locking on hers. 'I feel you in my arms,' he said. 'I feel your body wrap itself tightly around me. You feel it too, don't you, Bella? You feel me driving into you. You feel it right now: hard. Thick. Strong.'

She swallowed tightly. 'Why are you *doing* this?'

He leaned back in his chair and picked up his wine. 'I want you.'

She gave him a haughty glare. 'I'm not yours to have.'

His eyes challenged hers in a hot little tussle that had her spine tingling like high-voltage electricity. 'You've always been mine, Bella,' he said. 'That's why you hate me so much. You don't want to admit how much you want me. It shames you to think you lust after a bad boy with no pedigree. It's not done in your high-brow circles, is it? You're not supposed to slum it with the ill-bred. You're supposed to mingle your blood with the high flyers, but you just can't help yourself, can you? You want me.'

'I would rather boil in oil,' she said looking down her nose at him. 'You have no right to speak to me this way. I've done nothing to encourage you to think I...I fancy you.' *Or at least not since I was a silly little sixteen-year-old.* 'You have no place in my life. You never have and you never will.'

He leaned back in his chair with an indolent look. 'I'm at the centre of your life, baby girl,' he said. 'You can't do a thing without me. I could cut off your allowance right here and now if I thought it was warranted.'

Bella felt her heart slam against her ribcage. 'You can't do that.' *Please God, you can't do that.*

'You need to have another look at the fine print on your father's will,' he said. 'Why don't you check it out? I have the number of the lawyer in my phone.'

Bella looked at the mobile phone he was holding up. She swallowed once, twice. She suspected he wouldn't have said it if it wasn't true. Her father's will *was* incredibly complicated. She had read it years ago but it had been full of the sort of legalese that made it almost indecipherable. The financial-guardianship arrangement with Edoardo only made it a thousand times worse. 'What do I have to do to prove I'm old enough to make my own decisions, including choosing the man I want to marry?' she asked.

He studied her features for a moment, his gaze unnervingly steady on hers. 'I have no problem with you marrying,' he said. 'I just want to be sure you're doing it for the right reasons.'

She frowned at him. 'What other reason could there be other than I love him and want to spend the rest of my life with him?'

'People get married for lots of reasons,' he said. 'Mutual convenience, sharing familial wealth, arrangements between families—to name just a few.'

'Why is it so hard for you to accept that I'm truly in love?' she asked.

'What do you love about him?'

Bella found his direct look rather confronting. It made her feel as if he was seeing right inside her to where she kept her insecurities stashed away. She didn't want to be questioned on her love for Julian. She just loved him. He was perfect for her; he made her feel special.

He made her feel *safe*.

She shifted her gaze to the left of Edoardo's and answered, 'I love that he devotes so much of his time and energy to people less fortunate. He cares about people. All people. He can talk to anyone. It doesn't matter if they're rich or poor. He makes no distinction.'

There was a ticking silence.

'Anything else?' he asked.

She moistened her dry lips. 'I love that he loves me and he's not afraid to say it.'

'Words are cheap,' he said. 'Anyone can say them. The point is whether there's any truth in them in their actions.'

Bella gave him a direct look of her own. 'Have you ever been in love?'

His mouth cocked up at one side as if he found the notion amusing. 'No.'

'You seem very certain about that.'

'I am.'

'Not even a teensy, weensy little crush?'

'No.'

'So you just have sex for the physical release it offers?' she asked.

His eyes seemed to heat and smoulder the longer they held hers. 'It's the only reason I have sex.' He paused for a beat as his gaze continued to stoke hers. 'What about you?'

Bella felt a tremor of unruly forbidden desire roll through her like a bowling ball pitched down a steep descent. Her body shook and sizzled with it, every sensitive nerve suddenly awake and alert. She shifted in her seat, crossing her legs under the table, but if anything it concentrated the wicked sensations in the secret heart of her. It was as if he had a direct line to her womanhood by just looking at her. He was stroking her with his gaze, making love to her with his mind. She could see it in his expression—the knowing curve of his sensual lips and the slightly hooded gaze as it focused on her mouth.

She felt his kiss as surely as if he had closed the distance between them and pressed his mouth to hers. Her lips buzzed and tingled. Her tongue grew restless inside her mouth in its hunger to feel his mate with it. Her breasts felt full and sensitive behind the lace of her bra. Her knickers were damp. She could feel the moisture seeping from her and wondered if he had any idea of how much sensual power he had over her.

Of course he did.

'You haven't answered my question.'

Bella felt a blush steal across her cheeks. 'That's because it's none of your business.'

'You asked me first,' he pointed out. 'Fair's fair, and all that.'

She pressed her lips together for a moment. 'Sex is an important part of an intimate relationship,' she said. 'It's a chance to connect on both a physical and emotional level. It builds a stronger bond between two people who care about each other.'

'You sound like you just read that from a text-book,' he said, his mouth still cocked mockingly. 'How about you tell me what you *really* think?'

Bella felt her flush deepen. It seemed to spread all over her body. She felt hot. *Scorching hot.* She had never had a conversation like this with anyone, not even with one of her girlfriends.

Sex was something she'd had to work at. She had never felt all that comfortable with her body. She had spent most of the time during sex worrying if the cellulite on her thighs was showing or whether her partner was comparing her breasts to other women's.

As for her pleasure, well, that was another thing she wasn't too confident about. She had never been able to have an orgasm with a partner. She just wasn't able to relax or feel comfortable enough to let herself go.

That was why Julian had been such a refreshing change from her previous dates. He had never pressured her for sex. He had told her he was celibate and intended to stay that way until he was married. He had made a promise to God, and he was going to keep it. She had found that so endearing, so admirable, she had decided he would be the perfect husband for her.

'I think sex means different things to different people,' she finally said. 'What's right for one person might not be right for another. It's all a matter of feeling comfortable enough to express yourself in a…sexual way.'

'How do you know if you'll be comfortable with this Julian fellow?' he asked.

Bella picked up her wine glass for something to do with her hands. 'Because I know he'll always treat me with the utmost respect,' she said. 'He believes sex is God's gift to be treasured, not something to be dishonoured by selfish demands.'

He gave a little snort. 'You mean he'll pray before he peels back the sheets on your wedding night.'

She gave him a withering look. 'You are *such* a heathen.'

'And you are a silly little fool,' he threw back.

'You haven't got a clue what you're getting yourself into. What if he's hiding who he really is? What if this celibacy thing is just a ruse to get his hands on your money?'

'Oh, for pity's sake.'

'I mean it, Bella,' he said, his blue-green gaze suddenly intense and serious. 'You are one of the richest young women in Britain. It's no wonder men are beating a steady path to your door.'

Bella froze him with her stare. 'I don't suppose it has ever occurred to you that it might be because of my dazzling beauty and vivacious personality?'

He opened his mouth as if he was about to say something but then closed it. He let out a long breath and pushed back a thick lock of his hair that had fallen forward on his forehead. 'Your beauty and personality are without question,' he said. 'I just think you need to be a little more objective about this.'

She sat back in her chair with a thump. 'Thus speaks the man who measures everything by checks and balances,' she said, rolling her eyes. 'Don't you do things sometimes just because it *feels* right?'

His eyes remained steady on hers. 'Gut feeling doesn't cut it with me,' he said. 'It's too easy to allow your emotional investment in something or someone to cloud your judgement. The heavier the investment, the harder it is to see things and people for what or who they are.'

'How did you get so cynical?' Bella asked.

His eyes moved away from hers as he reached to top up their wine glasses. The sound of the wine making a *glock-glock-glock* noise as it poured out of the bottle was deafening in the silence. 'Born that way,' he said.

'I don't believe that.'

He met her gaze, his mocking half-smile back in place. 'Still trying to save my sorry soul, Bella?' he asked. 'I thought you gave up on that little mission years ago.'

'Have you told *anyone* about your childhood? About where you came from?' she asked.

A mask slipped over his features like a dust sheet over a piece of furniture. 'There's nothing to tell.'

'You must have had parents,' she said. 'A mother, at least. Who was she?'

'Leave it, Bella.'

'You must remember something about your childhood,' Bella pressed on. 'You can't have blocked everything out. You weren't born a teenager with authority issues. You were once a baby, a toddler, a young child.'

He let out a short, impatient-sounding breath and reached for his glass. 'I don't remember much of my childhood at all,' he said and drank a deep mouthful of his wine.

Bella watched his Adam's apple go up and down. Even though his expression was masked, there was anger in the action as he swallowed the liquid—anger and something else she couldn't quite put her finger on. 'Tell me what you do remember,' she said.

The silence was long and brooding, the air so

thick it felt like the ceiling had slowly lowered, compressing all the oxygen.

Bella continued to search his features. The stony mask had slipped just a fraction. She could see the flicker of a blood vessel in his temple. The grooves beside his mouth deepened as if he was holding back a lifetime of suppressed emotion. His nostrils flared as he took a breath. His eyes hardened to granite. His fingers around his glass tightened until she could see the whitening of his knuckles.

'Why did you get kicked out of all those foster homes?' she asked.

His eyes collided with hers. They were dark with a glitter that made the backs of her knees go fizzy again. 'Why do you think I was kicked out?' he asked with a tilt of his lips that looked more like a snarl than a smile. 'I was a rebel. A lost cause. Bad to the core. Beyond salvation.'

Bella swallowed a thick knot in her throat. He was so intimidating when he was in this mood but she was determined to find out more about him. His enigmatic nature intrigued her. She had always found his aloof, keep-away-from-me manner compellingly attractive. 'What happened to your parents?' she asked.

'They died.' He said the words as if they meant nothing to him. He showed no emotion at all. Not even a flicker. His face was like a marble statue, a blank, impenetrable mask.

'So you were an orphan?' Bella prompted.

'Yeah, that's me.' He gave a little laugh as he swirled the contents of his glass. 'An orphan.'

'Since when?' she asked. 'I mean, how old were you when your parents died?'

It seemed like a full year before he spoke; Bella waited out each pulsing second of the long, protracted silence. It was a silent battle of wills, but somehow she suspected the battle was not between her and him. It was between two parts of himself: the aloof loner who didn't need anyone and the man behind the mask who secretly did.

'I don't remember my father,' he said with the same blank, indifferent expression.

'He died when you were a baby?' she guessed.

'Yes.' There was still no emotion. No grief or sense of loss.

Bella moistened her lips, waiting a beat or two before asking, 'What happened?'

At first she didn't think he was going to answer. The silence stretched and stretched interminably.

'Motorbike accident,' he finally said. 'He wasn't wearing a helmet. Can't have been pretty.'

Bella winced. 'What about your mother?'

A tiny, almost imperceptible spasm tugged at the lower quadrant of his jaw. 'I was five,' he said and twirled his wine again, his eyes staring down at the liquid as it splashed against the sides of the glass.

'What happened to her?'

'She died.'

'How?'

There was another silence before he spoke. A bruised silence. 'Suicide.'

She gasped. 'Oh, my God, that's terrible.'

He gave a careless shrug. 'It wasn't much of a life for her once my father died.' He tipped back his head and drained his glass, setting it down on the table with a little thump.

Bella frowned as she thought of him as a young motherless boy. She had been totally devastated when her mother had driven away that day, but at least she had known her mother was still alive. How had Edoardo coped with losing his mother so young? 'Your father was Italian, wasn't he?'

'Yep.'

'And your mother?'

'English,' he said. 'She met my father while on a working holiday in Italy.'

'Who looked after you after she died?'

He put his napkin next to his plate and pushed back from the table, his expression closing like a door that had been clicked shut on a sliver of a view. 'Fergus needs to go outside,' he said. 'He's too stiff to use the pet door now.'

Bella sat back with a frown pulling at her forehead as she watched him stride from the room. He had told her things she was almost certain he hadn't even told her father. Her father had said Edoardo had always refused to speak of his early childhood and he wasn't to be pressured to reveal things he didn't want to reveal. She, like her father, had assumed it had been because Edoardo was ashamed of his background, given that it was so different from theirs. His youth had been misspent on rebellious behaviour that had alienated him from the very people who had wanted to help him. He had used the very words the authorities would have used to describe him: a rebel, a lost cause, bad to the core, beyond salvation. Was he really all or any of those things? What had happened to make him so distrustful of people? What had made him the closed-off enigma he was today?

And why on earth did it matter to her to find out? It wasn't as if it was any of her business.

He was her enemy.

He hated her as much as she hated him.

She chewed at her lower lip as she looked at his empty chair. It shouldn't matter to her what had happened to him. He had been surly and uncommunicative for as long as she had known him. He had clearly inveigled his way into her father's trust and taken control of her life. He had done nothing but taunt and ridicule her from the moment she had turned up at what used to be *her* house. He was threatening to ruin *her* wedding plans. He was the spanner in the works, the fly in the ointment, the brick wall she had to climb over or knock down.

It shouldn't matter… But somehow—rather surprisingly—it did.

CHAPTER FOUR

EDOARDO waited for Fergus to sniff every tree and shrub in the garden as the moon watched on with its wise and silent silver eye. The air was cold and fresh; the smell of the damp earth was like breathing in a restorative potion.

It cleared his head.

It *grounded* him.

It reminded him of how far he had moved from his previous life—a life where he'd had no control. No hope. Only pain and miserable, relentless suffering.

Haverton Manor was his sanctuary, the only place he had ever called home. The only place he had ever wanted to call home.

He clenched his fists and then slowly released them. The past was in the past and he should not have let Bella get under his skin enough to pick at the hard crust that covered what was left of his soul. Inside him were wounds he would allow *no one* to see. The scars he wore on the outside of his body were nothing to the ones on the inside. He could not bear pity. He could not stomach people's interest in what he wanted to forget. He didn't want to be painted as a victim. He had no time for people who saw themselves as victims.

He was a survivor.

He would not allow his past to cast a shadow over his future. He had proved all his critics wrong. He had made something of himself. He had used every opportunity Godfrey Haverton had offered him to better himself. He was educated. He was wealthy. He had everything he had ever dreamed of when he had been that cowering child shrinking away from the drunken blows of a cruel and sadistic stepfather. He had pictured his future in his head as a way to block out what was happening to him:

he had pictured the luxury cars, the lush, rolling fields of a country estate, the opulent mansion, the beautiful women and the designer clothes.

He had made it come true.

Haverton estate was his: every field and pasture, every hill and hillock, the lake, the woods and most importantly the manor—his very own regal residence, the ultimate symbol of having left his past well and truly behind.

No one would be able to take it off him. No one could toss him out on the street in the cold and wet. No one could deny him a roof over his head.

When he was a child he had dreamed of owning a place such as this. His very own fortress, his castle and his base. *His home.*

Godfrey had known how important the manor was to him: it was the first place he had felt safe. The first place he had put down roots. The first place he had discovered friendship and loyalty. Within these walls he had learned all he needed to learn in order to make something of his life. Before he had come here he had been close to giving up. He had gone beyond the point of caring what happened to him. But Godfrey had woken something in him with his quiet, patient way. He hadn't pressured him to open up. He hadn't bribed him or coerced him in any way. He had simply planted the seeds of hope in Edoardo's mind, seeds that had grown and grown until Edoardo had started to see the possibility of changing his life, becoming something other than a victim of circumstance and cruelty.

He was no longer that pitiful child with a constant fear of abandonment, with no one to turn to, with no one to love or be loved. He was no longer that brooding, resentful teenager with a chip on his shoulder.

He depended on *no one* for his happiness.

He had no need of anyone but himself. He was totally autonomous. He didn't want the ties and responsibilities that other people saw as a natural part of life. Marriage and children were not something he had ever pictured for himself. Life was too fickle for him to chance it. What if the same thing happened to him as had happened to his father—his life cut short in its prime and his wife and child left to fend for themselves as best they could, easy prey for the scurrilous, conscienceless predators out there who would do anything to get their hands on money for drugs and drink?

No. He was fine on his own; perfectly fine.

Bella was in the kitchen stacking the dishes into the dishwasher when Edoardo came back in. It was a domestic scene he wasn't used to seeing. She had never been one to lift a finger about the place. She had grown up with a band of willing servants to cater to her every whim. He had always thought her father had been far too lenient with her. She had never had to work for anything in her life. It had all been handed to her on a silver plate with the Haverton coat of arms emblazoned on it. She had flounced around issuing orders as if she was already lady of the manor, even as a small child. Not even as an adult had she ever considered the sacrifices Godfrey Haverton had made to provide a secure future for her. She hadn't even had the decency to be by his side as he drew his last, gasping breath.

He had been the one to watch Godfrey pass from life to death.

He had held his frail hand and listened to the sounds of the breath slowly leaving the old man's rail-thin body.

He had been the one to close Godfrey's eyes in final rest.

He had been the one to weep with grief at losing the one person on this earth who had truly believed in him. He had sworn on Godfrey's death bed that he would do the right thing by him and protect Bella. He would make sure she stayed out of trouble until the guardianship period was over. He would not let her waste her father's hard-earned money. And in the meantime he would continue to restore Haverton Manor into the grand old residence Godfrey had loved so much, thus keeping a part of his mentor and friend alive.

Bella closed the dishwasher and straightened, her tongue darting out to moisten her lips. 'I was going to make some coffee,' she said. 'Would you like some?'

Edoardo couldn't help a little lip curl. 'You mean you actually know how to boil water?'

She pursed her mouth and tossed the dishcloth she had been holding on the sink. 'I'm trying to be nice to you, Edoardo,' she said. 'The least you could do is meet me halfway.'

'Nice?' He gave a rough sound of derision. 'Is that what you call it? You're sucking up to me to get what you want.'

'I'm not,' she said. 'I've been thinking about what you told me about your parents—about being orphaned so young. I didn't understand how devastating it must have—'

'Cut it, princess,' he said savagely.

Her smooth forehead crinkled in a frown. 'But surely talking about it would be helpful?'

'There's nothing to talk about,' he said. He reached for the coffee grounds in the pantry and slammed them down on the counter. He filled the percolator with water, spooned in the coffee and switched it on, his hands clenching the counter until the tendons on the back stood out starkly against his tan. Was she never going to give this up? What was it about women that they had to *know* everything? To *talk* about everything? He wanted to block it out, not dredge it up all the time.

He wanted it to go away.

He *needed* it to go away.

The percolator hissed and spat in the silence.

Edoardo heard her move across the floor. She had such a light, almost silent tread but the hairs on the back of his neck lifted all the same. He felt her just behind him. He could smell her perfume. It danced around his nostrils. If she touched him, his control would snap. He could already feel it straining on its tight leash. It felt like a wild beast being held back by a thin, rusty chain. One of these days one of those fragile, corroded links would break.

He heard her draw in a small breath and then she spoke his name, softly and hesitantly. It was like a caress on his skin. It made every pore react as if a soft feather had brushed over him. 'Edoardo?'

He waited a beat before he turned around and looked down at her. Her beautiful heart-shaped face was uptilted and her big brown eyes were soft and dewy, her rosy lips full and moist. 'I know what you're doing,' he said with a cynical look. 'You always lay on the charm when you want something. I've seen you do it to your father hundreds of times. But you're wasting your time. It won't work with me.'

Her expression soured. 'Why must you be so...so *beastly*?' she asked.

'I won't be manipulated by you or anyone,' he

said. 'I made a promise to your father and I'm going to keep it.'

'I want to get married here,' she said, throwing him a combative look. 'I've dreamed of it all of my life. My father would have wanted it. You can't say he wouldn't.'

Edoardo thought of the highbrow, vacuous crowd she would have swarming around her like bees around a honey pot. The press would besiege the place. They would crawl over his private domain like ants at a picnic. His private sanctuary would become party central. And, if that weren't enough, he would have to watch Bella smiling up at some toffee-nosed man who—he could almost guarantee—only wanted her for her money. 'No,' he said. 'He wouldn't have wanted it, otherwise he would've left you the manor in the first place.'

She narrowed her eyes to hairpin-thin slits. 'You're doing this deliberately, aren't you?' she said. 'All that talk of wanting me was rubbish. You don't want me at all. You want the power.

It turns you on, doesn't it? You get off on it. You just want the rush it gives you to have me squirming in the palm of your uncivilised hand.'

Edoardo captured one of her wrists and held her fast. The urge to touch her had been unstoppable. He had barely even realised he had reached for her when he heard the gasp of her breath. He saw the sudden flare of her pupils. He felt the rapid jump of her pulse. He brought her closer, inch by inch, watching as her brown eyes went wider and wider. 'Maybe I should show you just how uncivilised I can be,' he drawled silkily.

Her pulse went wild beneath his fingers as he tugged her against his swollen groin. She swallowed and then licked her lips, her gaze tracking to his mouth as it came inexorably closer. He felt the soft gust of her breath against his lips. 'If you kiss me I will scratch your eyes out,' she said in a breathless little voice that was at odds with her warning.

'Before or after I kiss you?'

Her eyes blazed with hatred. 'During.'

He held her gaze for a throbbing heartbeat. 'I'd better not risk it, then,' he said, stepped back from her and reached for his keys on the hook near the door.

She blinked a couple of times as if she had been expecting him to call her bluff. 'Where are you going?' she asked.

He tossed the keys in the air before deftly catching them. 'Out.'

'Out where?' she asked with another frown. 'It's close to midnight.'

'Can you let Fergus out before you go to bed?' he asked. 'I might not get back before dawn.'

She gave him an irritated look. 'Is that how you stay under the press's radar?' she asked. 'By keeping your liaisons the other side of midnight?'

'Works for me,' he said, shouldering open the kitchen door.

She threw him a caustic glare. 'You disgust me.'

'Right back at you, princess,' he said and let the door swing shut behind him.

Bella was too annoyed to sleep. She tossed and turned and counted sheep and sheep dogs. She got up and had a glass of water. She checked on Fergus three times. She couldn't stop her mind from conjuring up images of Edoardo with one of his anonymous women. It disgusted her that he could just go out like that and find someone to slake his lust with. She could just imagine the type of woman he would go for: someone brash and bold, someone who would be confident sexually. His lovers wouldn't agonise over their breasts or thighs, they wouldn't worry about bikini waxes and whether they weren't responsive enough in his arms. He would *make* them respond just by looking at them, just like he did to her.

'Grrrhhh,' Bella said as she threw off the covers yet again.

She was out in the garden waiting for Fergus

to come back in when she saw the twin beams of Edoardo's car headlights move across the fields of the estate as he came up the long drive-way. 'Fergus?' she called out softly. 'Come on. Hurry up. I'm freezing to death out here.'

There was still no sign of the dog when Edo-ardo's car purred its way back to the garage. Bella listened as his footsteps crunched over the gravel of the driveway. She slunk against the shadows of the manor, holding the edges of her dressing gown tighter around her body. She didn't want him to think she had been losing sleep over his nocturnal activities. She didn't want him to think she had been waiting up for him to return, even though—subconsciously, at least—she had.

It was unnaturally, eerily quiet.

The night sounds that had seemed as loud as an orchestra rehearsing just moments ago had stilled as if silenced by a conductor's baton.

Bella edged her way along the manor with her back against the icy-cold, hard stone. Her skin was pebbled with goose bumps and her heart hammered like a piston. She inched her way closer to the window of the morning room. She took a breath and started to climb the trellis, where the gnarled and twisted skeleton of some clematis was situated, when a pair of strong arms suddenly tackled her from behind. 'Oomph!' she gasped as she fell backwards against a strong male body.

'Bella?' Edoardo swung her around and gaped at her in shock. 'What in God's name are you doing?'

She put up her hand in a little fingertip wave and gave him a sheepish smile. 'Hi…'

His expression went from shock to furious. 'What the hell are you playing at?' he asked. 'I could have hurt you. I thought you were a burglar.'

Bella straightened her dressing gown, which had slipped off one shoulder in the tussle. Her body was still tingling from where it had pressed against his. Her heart was still jumping and her pulse as crazy as an over-wound clock. 'Do you normally wrestle burglars to the ground?' she asked with a wry look.

He scraped a hand through his hair. 'Not usually.' He let his hand drop back by his side. 'Are you all right?'

'I will be when I get my heart to get back where it belongs,' she said with an attempt at humour. 'You scared the living daylights out of me. I didn't hear you make a sound. I thought you'd gone the other way around the house.'

'What on earth were you doing?' he asked, still frowning darkly.

'I was taking Fergus out for a comfort stop.'

'Then why hide in the shadows like an intruder?' he asked.

She gave a little shrug, suddenly feeling foolish and gauche. 'I didn't want you to see me…'

'Why not?'

She waved a hand over her night attire. 'I'm not…um, dressed.'

'I've seen you in a lot less,' he said.

Bella was glad of the muted moonlight because her face felt suddenly hot. 'So, how was your date?' she asked.

A shutter came down over his face. 'Where's Fergus?' he asked.

'Good question,' she said as she made her way back to the kitchen door. 'I was trying to find him when you came home. He's not very obedient, is he?'

'He's deaf and practically blind,' he said. 'You shouldn't have left him on his own. He gets disoriented at night.'

'You were the one who left him while you went off sowing your wild oats,' she tossed back. '*You* find him. I'm going back to bed.'

It was mid-morning when Bella came downstairs the next day. She supposed Edoardo had been up since dawn, or maybe he hadn't been to bed at all—or at least not his own bed, she thought with a niggle of pique.

She was halfway through a cup of tea and a

muffin when she heard a car come up the driveway. She went outside and watched as a slim, elegant woman of about thirty got out from behind the wheel.

'Hello,' the woman said with a friendly smile. 'You must be Bella. I'm Rebecca Gladstone. I moved into the area a few months ago.'

'Um…hi,' Bella said.

'Is Edoardo about?' Rebecca asked. 'I was passing and thought I should check on Fergus.'

'Fergus?'

Rebecca smiled. 'I'm the new vet.'

'Oh…' Bella pasted a stiff smile on her face. Was *this* Edoardo's latest lover? Beautiful, classy, educated, good with animals and probably children as well. She felt a tight pinching feeling close to her heart. Somehow she hadn't been expecting him to go for someone so…so likeable. Did this mean he would get married and fill Haverton Manor with a brood of kids and pets? He had stolen her house and now he had stolen her dream as well. It should be *her* children and *her* pets filling up the place, not his. 'Come this way,' she said. 'Fergus is asleep in the kitchen.'

Bella watched as Rebecca greeted the dog. Fergus, the old fool, practically gushed. His tail wagged like a metronome on steroids and he even gave a puppy-like wriggle of his hindquarters. Pathetic. Absolutely pathetic. 'He seems to really know you well,' Bella said.

'Yes, we're old friends, aren't we, Fergus?' Rebecca said, ruffling his ears.

Bella wanted to hate her but she couldn't quite do it. She decided to hate Edoardo a little bit more for choosing someone so damn perfect. Why couldn't he have a shallow, self-serving mistress she could really have a good bitch about?

After a minute or two, Rebecca stood up from examining the elderly dog. 'I'll leave some vitamins in case he's not eating properly,' she said, taking out a little bottle and placing it on the table. 'Irish wolfhounds don't live much longer than eight or so years. He's doing well for his age, but it's best to be on the safe side.'

Bella tried on another smile. 'Thanks.'

'So, how long are you staying for?' Rebecca asked.

'Just a few days,' Bella said. 'I haven't been home much just lately… Actually, not since my father's funeral.' *Not since he gave away my home to my worst enemy,* she added silently.

'I'm sure Edoardo will be glad of the company,' Rebecca said as she clipped shut her bag. 'He works far too hard, but I guess I don't have to tell you that.'

'I'm not sure Edoardo enjoys my company too much,' Bella said, pursing her mouth.

Rebecca looked at her quizzically. 'Oh? Why do you say that?'

Bella wished she hadn't been so transparent but it was a bit late to retract what she'd said. *In with a penny, in with a pound,* she thought. Anyway, why should she sugar-coat her relationship with Edoardo? He had probably derided her to Rebecca every chance he could. 'He thinks I'm a spoilt brat who hasn't grown up,' she said.

Rebecca studied her for a moment. 'You've known him a long time, then?'

'Since I was seven years old.'

'So you're like brother and sister?'

'Um…not quite,' Bella said, blushing in spite of every effort not to. She paused for a beat. 'We're not exactly bosom buddies.'

'He's your financial guardian, isn't he?' Rebecca said.

Bella felt like a fool. Who on earth had financial guardians these days? Kids under eighteen or elderly people with dementia, that was who. 'Yes,' she said. 'I expect Edoardo has told you all about it.'

Rebecca gave her a reassuring smile. 'It's all right,' she said. 'I didn't hear it from him. He never talks about you. I heard it from Mrs Baker. She told me your father set things up in a rather complicated fashion.'

'Very complicated,' Bella said, blowing out a breath. 'I can't do anything without Edoardo's approval. It's incredibly annoying.'

'I'm sure he would never stop you doing anything you really wanted to do,' Rebecca said. 'Anyway, it won't be long, and you'll be free to do what you like. I seem to remember Mrs Baker saying it's only until you turn twenty-five.'

'Or until I marry.'

'Are you planning on doing that any time soon?' Rebecca asked, glancing at Bella's left hand.

'It's not official as yet,' Bella said. 'I'm just waiting until he gets back from a trip abroad before we announce anything.'

'Congratulations,' Rebecca said. 'You must be so excited.'

'I am,' Bella said. *Or I would be, if it weren't for Edoardo standing in the way of my plans.*

There was the sound of firm footsteps, and Bella watched as Rebecca Gladstone's cheeks took on a pink hue as Edoardo strode in. He glanced at the dog in the basket before meeting Rebecca's gaze. 'What's going on?' he asked.

'I was in the area and thought I'd drop by,' Rebecca said. 'I've left some vitamins for Fergus. They'll boost his immune system.'

'Thank you,' Edoardo said. 'How much do I owe you?'

'Isn't it me who owes you?' Bella said with a pointed look. 'He was my father's dog, after all.'

'You don't owe me a thing, either of you,' Rebecca said. 'That's just a sample pack in any case.' She smiled up at Edoardo. 'Want to walk me to my car?'

His expression was as blank as a sheet of paper. 'Sure.'

'It was lovely to meet you, Bella,' Rebecca said. 'I hope you enjoy your stay.'

'I will,' Bella said with a smile that cracked her face.

'She's in love with you,' Bella said as soon as Edoardo came inside a few minutes later.

He reached for a glass and filled it with water from the tap. 'And you can tell that how, exactly?' he asked.

'She blushed as soon as you came into the room,' she said.

He turned from the sink to look at her. 'Just because a woman blushes doesn't mean she's in love,' he said. 'Take you, for instance.' He let his eyes run over her slowly but thoroughly. 'I could make you blush within seconds. Does it mean you're in love with me?'

Bella jerked her chin back against her neck in disdain, her cheeks feeling like they had been too close to a fire. 'I would never fall in love with someone like you.'

'That's very reassuring,' he said with a mocking slant of his mouth.

'Rebecca seems a very nice person,' she said. 'The least you could've done is said a proper hello to her.'

'I don't like impromptu visitors,' he said. 'If

she wanted to see me, all she had to do was call me and arrange a time.'

'Maybe she doesn't like being called in the middle of the night to suit your needs.'

He gave a loose shrug. 'She's not my type.'

'No, because she's got a brain between her ears,' she shot back. 'I can only imagine what your type is like: big boobs, toothpaste-commercial smile, long legs and no conversation. Am I close?'

A half-smile kicked up the edges of his mouth. 'Close enough,' he said.

'Have you dated her?' she asked.

'We had a drink a few weeks back,' he said.

'Have you slept with her?'

'No.'

'Why not?' she asked.

He put the glass down on the counter. 'What's with all the questions?' he asked. 'Are you jealous?'

'Of course I'm not jealous!' Bella retorted. 'I just think you could really hurt her if you don't do the right thing by her.'

'It's not my problem.'

'It *is* your problem,' she said. 'You should nip it in the bud before she gets too involved. You shouldn't encourage her to just drop by if you're not serious about her.'

'I didn't encourage her to drop by,' he said. 'I've given her no encouragement, full-stop.'

Bella folded her arms across her chest. 'She obviously thinks you have,' she said.

'Then she's mistaken.'

'Is she who you went to last night?' she asked.

'No.'

'Who *did* you see?'

He leaned back against the counter in an indolent fashion. 'Are you sure you're not jealous?' he asked.

She rolled her eyes. 'How could I be?' she asked. 'I'm about to get engaged.'

'It's not official.'

'It will be soon.'

'There's been nothing in the press about your

relationship with your preacher boy,' he said. 'Not even a whisper.'

'That's because Julian doesn't attract press attention,' she said. 'Anyway, I want to wait until he gets back from Bangladesh before we tell anyone anything. I'm going to meet his family and then we're going to make a formal announcement.'

'You're assuming, of course, that I'll agree to this match.'

Bella unfolded her arms and clenched her fists. 'You can't prevent me from marrying the man I love.'

His blue-green eyes challenged hers. 'If you love him so much then why aren't you over there with him?' he asked.

Bella floundered for a moment. 'I…I have things to see to here,' she said. 'I'd be in the way over there. I need to learn the ropes a bit before I go with him on a mission.'

He made a sound of scorn in his throat. 'I

just can't see you handing out trinkets to the natives.'

'That's not what missionaries do these days,' she said. 'They help to build schools and hospitals.'

'And what will you do when you do accompany him?' he asked.

'I'll support him in any way I can,' she said.

'It's what every man of the cloth needs,' he said with a curl of his lip. 'A rich wife to bankroll every do-good project.'

Bella glowered at him. 'You think I haven't got a clue, don't you? You think I'm too stupid to do anything but get my nails done.'

'You're not stupid,' he said. 'You're naïve. You've lived a sheltered life. You don't know how the other half lives. You don't know how desperate and ruthless people can be.'

'Like you, you mean?' she said with an arch look.

His eyes glinted as they locked down on hers.

'I can be very ruthless when I go after something I want.'

Bella felt the skin of her arms lift in a tiny shiver. 'You can't always have everything you want,' she said.

The corner of his mouth lifted in a devilish smile. 'Who's going to stop me?' he asked.

She quickly moistened her parchment-dry lips, her heart doing double time inside her ribcage. 'I'm not going to sleep with you, Edoardo.'

He picked up a lock of her hair and coiled it around his finger. She felt the gentle pull on her scalp; it made her backbone tingle and fizz like an effervescent liquid was being poured down its length. 'I'm not planning on us doing too much sleeping once I have you in my bed,' he said.

Bella's insides flickered and flashed with red-hot lust. She felt shocked at her involuntary response to his incendiary words. After years of keeping her distance, her body now seemed to have a mind of its own. It totally disregarded her common sense. Her body was drawn to him, lured into his sensual orbit like a satellite.

'Read my lips, Edoardo,' she said stiffly. 'I am *not* going to end up in bed with you, asleep or not.'

He slowly unwound her hair, his eyes meshed with hers in a sensual lock that felt like an intimate caress at the secret heart of her femininity. 'Want to put money on that, princess?'

Bella gave her head a toss as she stepped away from him. 'I don't need to,' she said. 'I already know who's going to win.'

'So do I,' he said and, before she could get in the last word, he left.

CHAPTER FIVE

BELLA kept out of Edoardo's way for the next couple of days. She caught up with some old friends in the village and ate out rather than spend time alone with him at the manor.

But as the week drew to a close, she felt increasingly bored and restless. She hadn't heard from Julian, as he had gone to a new mission in the mountains where the telephone signal was poor. With each day that passed without a message from him, she felt more insecure. She needed his reassurance and encouragement. She needed his enthusiasm and positive attitude to life.

A niggling doubt had started playing at the corners of her mind about how she would fit into his life of self-sacrifice. She admired his commitment and faith enormously, but she sometimes wondered if he could be passionate about anything other than trying to save the world. She knew it was selfish of her to want to be the central focus of his attention, but she couldn't help wondering if he truly loved her the way she wanted to be loved.

Her mother's desertion when she was so young had made her insecure about intimate relationships. She loved too deeply and too quickly, only to be disappointed when the other party pulled away from her. Was Julian's trip abroad his way of distancing himself? She knew he loved her, but it wasn't a passionate all-or-nothing love.

It was a *safe* love.

A love she could count on to get her through the bad times as well as the good. A love that would be the solid foundation of a well-ordered family life.

It was what she wanted. What she *needed*. She didn't want to be like her mother, flitting off to somewhere exotic on yet another passionate fling that would only end in tears and heartbreak.

She didn't want the hair-raising, nail-biting, gut-twisting rollercoaster ride of passion. She wanted the smooth, predictable ride of a merry-go-round.

Bella was in the kitchen poking about in the fridge when Edoardo came in from outside.

'Eating in tonight?' he asked as he hung up his jacket on the hook behind the door.

She closed the fridge guiltily. 'I can get something later,' she said.

'I can rustle up something for both of us,' he said. 'You don't have to hide away in your room.'

'I'm not hiding away in my room,' she said. 'I've been busy catching up with friends.'

He grunted and moved across to wash his hands at the sink. 'Give me half an hour,' he said. 'I have to sort something out on my computer.'

'Who taught you to cook?' she asked.

He dried his hands on some paper towels and dropped them in the pedal bin. 'No one in particular,' he said. 'I didn't stay anywhere long enough to pick up more than the basics.'

'What was the longest you stayed with a foster family?'

Edoardo felt the familiar tension crawl over his skin like a cockroach. He hated thinking about his past, let alone talking about it. He wanted to forget it had ever happened. He wanted it erased from his brain. He mostly *had* erased it from his mind. Every time Bella pushed him for more information, it made his head ache with the suppressed memories. They felt like they were busting out of the shackles he had bound them with all those years ago. 'Can you quit it with the twenty questions?' he said. 'I'm not in the mood for it.'

'You're never in the mood,' she said. 'You're like a closed book. Lots of people come from difficult backgrounds. I don't see why you have to be so secretive about it.'

He stepped into her body space, watching as her big brown eyes rounded. 'You're playing with fire,' he warned. 'But I think you already know that, don't you?'

A silence throbbed between them.

'I've known you since I was a child, but I hardly know you at all,' she said in a husky tone.

He placed his hands on her shoulders and watched as the tip of her tongue snaked out to sweep over her lips. He had never seen a more kissable mouth. Desire twisted and tightened in his groin. He felt his body surge and swell. He wanted her so badly it was like a drug his system craved. The trouble was, he knew one taste would never be enough. He wasn't sure how long with her would be enough. For years he had thought of this moment, when she would come to him with that look of wanting in her eyes. He saw it: the need, the lust and the longing. It pulsed in the air in a hot, swirling current that was almost palpable.

Her eyes flickered to his mouth and back again to his. 'I want to know who you are,' she said. 'Who you *really* are.'

'This is who I really am,' he said.

'I want to know why you're so closed off emotionally,' she said. 'You push everyone away. Why do you do that?'

Edoardo gripped her shoulders a little tighter. 'I'm not pushing you away right now, am I? In fact, I'm about to bring you a whole lot closer.'

He felt her body brush against his. It engulfed his in a wave of hot longing that was like wildfire as he pulled her against him, male against female, need against need. His mouth came down slowly, giving her plenty of time to get away if she wanted to—but she didn't move. Instead, she parted her lips as his came down. He brushed the point of his tongue against hers, a teasing taste of the eroticism to come. He felt her whole body respond. She pressed close and whimpered in the back of her throat as his tongue teased her again, in and out, barely touching, just hinting at the sensual delight in store.

Her tongue flickered against his, flirting, daring, increasingly provocative. Her hands snaked up around his neck, her fingers weaving through his hair, her pelvis jammed against his. His erection became painful as it moved against her urgently. She rubbed against him wantonly, her body pliant and soft against his.

Edoardo devoured her mouth like a starving man does a succulent meal. He fed off her hot, sweet moistness, tasting the nectar of her; relishing in the answering dart and dance of her tongue as it met and mated with his.

She was everything and more than he had dreamed of: sweet yet sultry, shy yet demanding. He couldn't get enough of her softness. She yielded to his pressure, softly whimpering in delight as he drove deeper and deeper, demanding more and more of her with each thrust or flicker of his tongue against hers.

Her perfume danced around his nostrils, teasing him, tantalising him with the scent of hot summer nights. He was almost dizzy with it, intoxicated.

He moved his hands from her shoulders and splayed them roughly in her silky hair. Her slender hips moved against his, instinctively searching for him. Wanting him as a woman wants a man.

He ached to feel her surround him, to milk him of his essence with every tight contraction of her body. The need inside him built to fever pitch. Had he ever wanted someone as much as this? It was like a raging torrent in his blood. He could think of nothing but how much he wanted to possess her. His body was rigid with desire, hot and pulsing against her.

His right hand moved under her top to cup her breast through the lace of her bra, the softness and delicate shape of her thrilling him. That night in the library she had brazenly taunted him with her body. But it was her touch that had unravelled his control. The sexy little tiptoe of her fingers on his chest had been like throwing a match on a spill of gasoline. It had roared through his veins until he had finally snapped and grabbed her and shown her what a real man felt like instead of those pasty-faced adolescents she had surrounded herself with like a queen bee with drones.

He had wanted her then and he wanted her now.

He pushed her bra aside and bent his head to take her nipple in his mouth, swirling his tongue around and around until she was groaning in delight, her fingers digging into his waist for purchase.

He moved to her other breast, taking his time exploring it in intimate detail: the tightly budded nipple, the pink areola and the sensitive underside where thousands of nerves quivered and danced under his touch.

Her hands moved from his waist and danced over the front of him. His erection jutted proudly against her tentative touch, the blood thundering in him—the ache of need so intense he felt like a teenager at his first sexual encounter.

He reclaimed her mouth and backed her up until she was against the kitchen table. He lifted her onto it, and she opened her thighs and wrapped her legs around him, her arms tight around his neck as her greedy little mouth wreaked havoc on his.

The kiss went on and on, drawing him into a sensual whirlpool that was making it impossible to think of anything but possessing her totally. His erection was nudging her intimately, the damp barrier of her lacy knickers taunting him until he was fit to explode.

He blindly went in search of her slick wetness, pushing aside the cobweb of lace so he could slip one finger inside. He felt the tight grip of her body, heard her little gasp of pleasure. But then she jolted and pulled back from him, her cheeks fire-engine red, her eyes shocked and wide with horror. 'Stop!' she said.

He gave her a questioning look. 'Stop?'

She pushed at his chest with both of her hands. 'Get away from me!'

He stepped back and watched as she scrambled off the table and pushed her skirt down with shaking hands. She kept her gaze averted, her shoulders hunched as she wrapped her arms around her body. 'You had no right to do that,' she said.

'To kiss you?' he asked.

She threw him a blistering look. 'You shouldn't have touched me…like that.'

'Why not?' he asked.

She frowned fiercely at him. 'You know why not.'

'Because you fancy yourself in love with another man?'

Her cheeks fired up again. 'You went too far,' she said. 'You know you did.'

'So,' he said with a sardonic look. 'You're OK

with me kissing you, but it's hands off below the waist. Is that it?'

She compressed her lips until they lost their rosy tint. 'That shouldn't have happened either,' she said, still frowning furiously. 'Although I accept it was partly my fault.'

'Partly?' He gave a scornful grunt. 'That was the biggest come-on I've had since you flashed your breasts at me when you were sixteen.'

'I wasn't giving you the come-on back then,' she said in a tight little voice.

'So what *were* you doing?'

She shifted her gaze. 'I was angry with you. You were always ignoring me as if I was just a silly little spoilt brat who was always getting in the way. I wanted to teach you a lesson.'

'You wanted me to notice you,' he said. 'Well, here's the thing, princess—I noticed you. I noticed everything about you. I just didn't follow you around with my tongue hanging out like all of your pimply suitors.'

Her eyes came back to his, the colour still

heightened in her cheeks. 'Can we just forget this ever happened?' she asked.

Edoardo let the silence be his answer.

She swallowed a couple of times, an agitated look in her eyes. 'It meant nothing,' she said. 'It was probably just hormones or something. It happens to women as well as men, you know.'

'Lust.'

She gave him an irritated frown. 'Do you have to be so…blunt?'

'No point dressing it up in fancy euphemisms,' he said. 'You've got the hots for me. I'm gagging for you. The thing is, what are we going to do about it?'

'Nothing,' she said, folding her arms even tighter across her chest. 'We're going to do nothing, because it's wrong.'

He gave her a wicked smile. 'I won't tell anyone if you don't.'

She flung herself away. 'I'm going to bed. Goodnight.'

He waited until she was almost out of the door

before he spoke. 'If you can't sleep, you know where to find me. I'll be happy to be of service.'

She gave him an arctic blast with her gaze by way of answer and then disappeared.

Bella was still shaking with reaction when she got to her bedroom. She closed the door and wished there was a lock on it. Not for Edoardo, but for herself. She didn't trust herself not to wander down the long corridor to where his bedroom was and take him up on his offer to "service" her.

She groaned in self-recrimination. How could she have been so stupid to get so close to him again? He had danger written all over him; it was like a tattoo on his body only she could see.

His touch had set her flesh alight. She had not been able to control her reaction to him. It had taken over her common sense, her principles and morals.

She had wanted him.

She *still* wanted him.

The pulse of her blood was still reverberating through her body like a tiny bell struck by a sledgehammer. She could still feel where his long, thick finger had been. If she squeezed her thighs together, she could recreate the delicious sensation of him touching her so boldly, so possessively. And that was just his finger! What if he were to…?

No.

She slammed the brakes on her traitorous imaginings. She could not, *would* not, go there. He was off-limits for a host of reasons.

He was her enemy.

He only wanted her to prove a point.

She was a trophy he wanted to collect just like a big-game hunter. He would hang her up on his wall of sexual conquests. He would mock her as soon as he had finished with her.

He didn't have a heart. He was not capable of feeling anything for her other than lust.

Bella wrenched herself out of her clothes, tossing them to the floor as she stomped to the *en suite*. But showering did nothing to quell the aching, pulsing need of her flesh. If anything, it made it worse. She was hyper-aware of her body, of all its nerves and sensations and needs. It was as if her skin had turned itself inside out.

She wrapped herself in a towel and went back to her bedroom, but it was impossible to even think of sleeping. She looked at the bed, and her brain immediately conjured up an image of Edoardo lying there waiting for her. He was so tall he would have taken up most of the mattress. In his arms downstairs she had felt tiny and dainty, feminine and all hot, sensual woman.

She imagined him naked on her bed, his muscled body lean, cut, carved and *aroused*.

She let out a stiff curse, veered away from the bed and looked out of the window. The moon was high in the sky, casting a silvery glow over the rolling fields. She rested her forehead against the glass of the window and closed her eyes and groaned.

She heard a sound of a door opening and closing downstairs and opened her eyes. She watched as Edoardo took Fergus outside for his last comfort stop. He waited near the parterre garden, his tall figure so still and silent as the dog went about his business in the shadows.

Bella was transfixed.

The moonlight captured Edoardo's arresting features in relief. He looked like a dark knight or warrior fighting some internal battle of his own. His jaw was locked tight and his fists were thrust into the pockets of his trousers. His broad shoulders were fixed in position, the length of his spine straight and grimly determined. His brow was heavily furrowed, tense in fierce concentration.

Then, as if he sensed her watching him, he turned and locked gazes with her.

Bella felt the shock of the visual connection like a punch to her solar plexus. Her heart kicked like a horse's hoof against her breastbone. Her breathing stalled and her mouth went dry.

His eyes read her mind as surely as his hands and mouth had read her body only half an hour ago.

She jumped back from the window like someone leaping away from a roaring blaze. She clutched at her chest, sure her heart was going to flop like a goldfish tossed out of its bowl and land on the carpet at her feet.

What was *wrong* with her?

She wasn't a teenage girl experiencing her first crush. She was an adult, a mature, sensible adult who was about to become engaged to a man she loved and admired. She had no right to be lusting after a man she didn't even like.

It was shocking.

It was immoral.

It was *tempting*.

She grabbed twin handfuls of her hair and castigated herself. 'No. No. No.'

She heard the stairs creaking as Edoardo's

firm tread came up to her floor. Her heart skipped another beat. She held her breath, her body poised, every nerve super-alert, her self-control and resolve gone to some far-off place she couldn't access even if she wanted to.

But then there was silence.

Nothing but an empty, hollow silence, apart from the lone hooting of an owl as it flew past her window, the sound of its wings moving through the air like a velvet cape being swished around someone's shoulders.

CHAPTER SIX

BELLA wasn't sure what woke her. She hadn't even realised she had been asleep, but she must have been because when she opened her eyes and checked the clock, it was close to four in the morning. She pushed back the covers and sat up, straining her ears in the eerie silence.

She didn't hear a thing for a full minute or so and then she heard a faint groan. Her skin lifted in goose bumps, as if a ghost's hand had touched her.

Don't be silly, she chided herself as she reached for her wrap. *Haverton Manor does not have any resident ghosts.* At least, none that she knew of.

She tiptoed out into the corridor and immediately noticed a sliver of muted light shining from beneath Edoardo's door at the other end of the passage. She chewed at her lip, wondering if it was wise to go any further. But then she heard the groan again, louder this time, and it was definitely coming from inside his room.

She pushed her reservations aside and padded down to his door, softly tapping on it as she leant her ear to the woodwork. 'Edoardo?' she said. 'Are you all right?'

There was a rustle of sheets being wrestled with. 'Go back to bed,' he said, but his voice didn't quite have the stern authority she was used to hearing in it.

She turned the doorknob before she could change her mind and stepped over the threshold. Her eyes went to his figure lying in a tangle of sheets, the pallor of his face almost the same shade of white. 'Are you ill?' she asked.

He cranked open one eye and told her to get out with an expletive graphically sandwiched between the curt command.

Bella turned on the major light near the door

but he immediately swore again and put his forearm across his eyes. 'Turn off the damn light!' he growled.

She flicked the switch off and came over to the bed where the light from his bedside lamp was shining with a pallid glow. 'What's wrong?' she asked.

'Get the hell out of here.'

'But you're sick.'

'I'm fine,' he said through gritted teeth.

Bella rolled her eyes and leaned forward to put a hand on his brow but he must have sensed her coming for him and blocked her by grabbing her wrist with his other hand. He opened his eyes to narrow squints and glared at her. 'I told you to get the hell out of here.'

She felt the bruising crush of his fingers around her wrist and winced. 'You're hurting me.'

He dropped her wrist. 'Sorry.' He let out a serrated sigh and covered his eyes again. 'Just leave me alone…please?'

Bella sat gently on the edge of the bed next to his thighs. 'Migraine?' she asked softly.

His whole body sank against the mattress. 'It'll pass,' he said on another weak sigh. 'They always do.'

'You get them often?'

'Now and again.'

'I've never seen you sick before,' she said.

He cranked open one eye again. 'Enjoy the show,' he said dryly.

She placed a hand on his brow, frowning at how clammy it was. 'Have you taken anything for it?' she asked.

'Paracetamol.'

'That's hardly going to do much,' she said. 'You need something stronger. What if I call an after-hours doctor?'

'No.'

'But—'

'No,' he said, glaring at her again. 'Will you quit it with the sweet little nurse routine and get the hell out?'

'I'm not leaving you like this,' she said. 'You could fall and knock yourself out or something.'

He flopped back down, but within a few seconds he suddenly reared up and, almost shoving her aside, stumbled to the *en suite*, not even stopping to close the door. Bella winced in empathy as he was violently, wretchedly sick. She gently pushed the door back, rinsed a face cloth under the tap and silently passed it to him where he was huddled over the toilet bowl.

'You don't give up easily, do you?' he said but there was no sting in it.

'I choose my battles,' she said and rinsed out another face cloth.

He took it from her once he had flushed the toilet. 'Thanks,' he said a little gruffly.

'My pleasure.'

He gave her a look. 'I bet you're enjoying this.'

Bella frowned at him. 'Why would I enjoy seeing you, or anyone, suffer?'

He hauled himself upright and took a moment to steady himself against the basin. She could see the outline of every muscle of his back and shoulders beneath the thin cotton T-shirt he was wearing. The boxer shorts left most of his long legs bare, the muscles strongly corded with regular and strenuous exercise. 'There are people in this world who would enjoy nothing more,' he said with a bitter twist of his mouth. 'It's sport for them. Cheap entertainment.'

'I hope I never meet someone like that,' she said, giving an involuntary shudder.

He looked at her for a long moment. She sensed he was looking at her but not actually seeing her. His eyes had a far-away look, a shadowed look. But then he blinked, turned away and moved back to the bedroom on legs that didn't seem all that steady.

Bella came up alongside him and put an arm around his lean waist. 'Here,' she said. 'Let me help you.' She led him back to the bed and, while he was still standing, quickly straightened the mangled linen.

He closed his eyes once he was lying flat. 'If

you tell anyone about this, I'll have to kill you,' he said after a moment's silence.

She smiled, and before she could stop the impulse, she briefly touched the ends of her fingers against his where they were lying on the mattress close to her thigh. 'You'll have to catch me first.'

He gave a soft little grunt without opening his eyes. 'That will be the easy part,' he said and within half a minute he was soundly asleep.

Bella woke again as the sun touched her face in a golden slant from the window. She stretched her legs—and encountered a hair-roughened one. Her eyes flew open as she realised she was in bed with Edoardo.

You're in bed with Edoardo Silveri!

The words were like a neon sign flashing inside her head.

Had she *slept* with him? Had she actually *had sex* with him? She squeezed her thighs together and was momentarily reassured. But why, then, was she lying in his arms with her legs caught up with his?

OK, let's be sensible about this, she thought. There's got to be a perfectly reasonable explanation for why she was lying with her legs entangled with his. She was still in her piglet pyjamas. All the buttons were still done up. Maybe she'd just drifted to sleep and unconsciously reached for him. Or maybe he had reached for her. Why, then, hadn't she woken up and moved out of reach?

Could she somehow wriggle away and leave without him waking?

Before she could get her scrambled thoughts together, he turned and looked at her.

'So you slept with me after all,' he said.

'I did not!'

He smiled a smile that tugged on something deep inside her belly, like a small needle pulling on a tiny thread. 'You did too,' he said. 'I heard you snoring.'

'I do *not* snore.'

He picked up a lock of her hair and slowly wound it around one of his fingers. She couldn't help noticing it was the same finger he had slipped inside her the evening before. She felt her inner core give a little tremor of remembered pleasure. 'You snuffle,' he said.

'Snuffle?' She wrinkled her nose. 'That doesn't sound much better.'

He gave her hair a gentle tug, his eyes holding hers in an erotic lock. 'Come here,' he commanded.

Bella let her breath out in a fluttery rush that felt like the pages of a book being rapidly thumbed inside her chest. 'Don't do this, Edoardo,' she said.

His eyes read the message her mind was relaying, not the one her mouth had just uttered so breathlessly. 'You want me,' he said. 'You curled yourself around me during the night. I could have taken you then and there.'

'I'm about to become engaged to another man,' Bella said, but right at that very moment she wasn't sure if she was reminding him or herself.

'Call it off.'

She looked at his mouth, her belly turning over itself as she thought of how it had felt to have those sensual lips moving against hers. She forced her gaze back to his blue-green one. 'I can't call it off,' she said. 'I don't *want* to call it off.'

He tugged on the tether of her hair; it was part pleasure and part pain. But wasn't that just typical of what she felt for him—a confusing mix of emotions she didn't want to examine in too much detail? She hated him and yet her body wanted him as it had wanted no one else. His mouth came closer and closer, stopping just above hers. 'I could talk you into it,' he said. 'All it would take is one little kiss.'

Bella put a finger against his lips, the graze of his stubble sending a dart of longing straight to her core. 'I can't.'

He opened his mouth and sucked her finger

into his mouth, gently snagging it with his teeth as his eyes held hers in a silent challenge that made her insides quiver like not-quite-set jelly.

A sweeping wave of red-hot desire coursed through her.

She felt her body gravitate towards him like a magnet attracting metal. Temptation was like a surging tide she had to swim against without the use of limbs. She felt the hard ridge of his erection against her belly and ached to hold it in her hand, to stroke him, to explore him, to *taste* him. Her hand moved forward but then she snatched it back, shocked at her own wantonness. 'Let me go,' she said, pulling at the lock of hair still tethered to his finger. 'Please?'

His eyes smouldered with unmet needs. She felt the echo of them like a drum beat in her body. He slowly unwound her hair until there was nothing connecting them but the desire that throbbed like soundwaves in the air.

He got off the bed and hauled the T-shirt he was wearing over his head.

'What are you doing?' Bella asked, pulling her knees up to her chest as she sat up on the bed.

'I'm going to have a shower,' he said and stepped out of his boxer shorts.

Her eyes widened at the sight of him so gloriously male and so potently aroused. She gulped and quickly covered her eyes with her hands. 'For God's sake, can you stop parading yourself around like a peacock?'

He gave a mocking laugh. 'Stop acting like a shy little virgin,' he said.

Bella didn't know why but she *felt* like a virgin when she was with him. His wealth of experience was so much broader than hers. She knew it just by looking at him. She *sensed* it in her body. He only had to look at her with those blue-green eyes of his and all her nerves and senses would go off like rescue flares.

She didn't open her eyes until she heard the *en suite* door close. She quickly scrambled off the bed and bolted, not stopping until her bedroom door was shut tight against the temptation of his touch.

* * *

Edoardo worked outdoors all day in spite of the freezing weather. He wanted Bella so badly it was like a persistent ache in his body. Lying next to her last night had been a form of torture. He had wanted to cover her body with his, to thrust into her softness and finally claim her as his. She had crawled all over him during the night, her soft little hands reaching for him, her warm, sweet breath dancing all over his chest as she snuggled close. It had been so hard not to peel those ridiculous pyjamas from her body and plant kisses all over her skin. He had wanted to explore her in intimate detail, to caress her breasts, to taste them again, to roll his tongue over those tight little nipples. He had wanted to slip his finger inside her hot moistness, to feel the delicious clench of her body, to taste her saltiness with his tongue.

But instead he had stared fixedly at the moonlight reflected on the ceiling as he had slowly run his fingers through the gossamer silk of her hair while she slept.

He never spent the whole night with anyone. It was a rule he had never broken. His nightmares were both terrifying and dangerous. He was always so frightened he might hurt someone by lashing out while he was reliving the horror of his childhood.

He loathed the weakness of his body. His migraines were not as frequent as they once had been but they more than made up for it when they came. Last night's had been the worst in a long while. The doctors had told him stress was a contributing factor. Bella pushing him for information about his childhood had been the trigger; he should never have allowed her to get under his guard like that. She had a way of slipping under his defences, ambushing him with her concerned looks and softly spoken words.

He could just imagine the shock and disgust on her face if he told her about his past. For all these years she had goaded him, taunted him with words about his background that were a whole lot closer to the truth than she probably realised.

He *felt* filthy. He had lived in filth so long he still felt dirty underneath his skin even though the outside was now clean.

He *felt* uncivilised. His childhood had been a black hole of despair. He had wanted to die at times rather than endure it. His anger and rage at the world had been like a cancer growing inside him. He had hit out at everyone. He hadn't trusted anyone to do the right thing by him. He could not afford to get his hopes up only to have them brutally dashed down again. It had been so much harder to summon the will to live after a let-down.

Bella had grown up with every privilege. She had never wanted anything she couldn't have had at the click of her finger. She had never had to fight to stay alive.

He was still fighting his demons. They plagued

him when he was awake and they tortured him when he was asleep.

Sometimes he wondered if he would ever be free.

It was late in the afternoon before Bella saw him again. She was coming back from a walk to the lake when she saw him up on a ladder doing something to one of the second-storey windows. She would have walked past without acknowledging him but the ladder shifted as he reached for one of the tools on his work belt, and her stomach suddenly lurched at the thought of him falling to the icy ground below. 'Do you need me to hold the ladder steady?' she said.

He gave her a brief glance and turned back to the task at hand. 'If you like.'

She watched from below as he shaved some wood off the casement with a plane. The muscles of his wrists and forearms bunched as he worked. He looked strong and fit and every inch a man in his prime. She tried not to think about what she had seen that morning but it was impossible to rid her mind of the image of his aroused body. Her insides were still smouldering with lust. She had been trying to ignore it all day but it was like a switch had been turned on inside her and she had no idea how to turn it off.

The ladder started to shudder again as he came down. She leaned her weight into it and only stepped away once he was safely down. 'What was wrong with the window?' she asked.

'Water damage,' he said, wiping some wood dust off his forehead with his forearm. 'We had a big snowfall a few weeks back. The wood's swollen with moisture. It'll need replacing eventually.'

'Why don't you get a professional to do this sort of stuff?' Bella asked.

'I enjoy it,' he said as he gathered his tools.

'That's beside the point,' she said. 'What if you had a fall? There would be no one around to help you. You could break your neck or something.'

His eyes met hers as he straightened. 'That would be quite convenient for you, wouldn't it?'

She frowned at him. 'What do you mean by that?'

'You'd get the manor back,' he said. 'That's what you'd like, isn't it?'

'It's my home,' she said, shooting him a resentful look. 'Generations of Havertons grew up here. I don't see why a blow-in like you should take it away from its rightful owner.'

'Not happy with your four-storey mansion in Chelsea and the millions of pounds in assets?' he asked.

She glowered at him. 'That's beside the point. This is where I grew up. This is where I expected my children to grow up. You don't belong here. I do.'

'Your father obviously thought differently,' he said.

'He should have consulted me about it,' Bella

said. 'The least he could have done is put it in both our names.'

'Would you have been happy living with me here?' he asked.

'No, I would not,' she said. 'Would you?'

'I don't know,' he said with a glinting smile. 'It could prove to be quite entertaining.'

She gave him a flinty look. 'I can assure you that if you get sick again I will not be racing to your aid in the middle of the night. You can jolly well fend for yourself.'

'Suits me.'

She pressed her lips together for a moment. 'Nor will I allow you to take advantage of me like you did this morning.'

'How did I take advantage of you?' he asked.

'You were in my bed.'

'Not because I wanted to be.'

His smile was arrogantly, *irritatingly* confident. 'No one forced you into it. You came of your own free will. And I have a feeling you'll be back before too long.'

Bella glared at him. 'Do you really think I'm that much of a pushover? I don't even like you. I hate you. I've always hated you.'

'I know, but that's why it will be such great sex,' he said. 'I can hardly wait to feel you come. I bet you'll go off like a bomb.'

Her cheeks fired with heat and she clenched her hands into fists. 'I am *not* going to have sex with you.'

He ran his eyes over her leisurely, heating her with the caress of his gaze as if he had physically touched her. She felt her breasts tingle, she felt her insides contract and shamelessly weep with want. 'It's going to happen,' he said. 'You can already feel it, can't you?'

'I feel nothing,' she bit out.

He took half a step to shrink the distance between their bodies. Bella had nowhere to move as the garden bed was behind her. She drew in a breath as he trailed a lazy finger across the sensitive skin stretched over her left clavicle. Her nerves leapt and danced and shimmied under his mesmerising touch. 'Can you feel that?' he asked, locking his gaze on hers.

She swallowed tightly as a host of sensations coursed through her like a shivery tide. 'You have no right to touch me,' she said, although her voice wasn't as strong and determined as she had intended. It sounded breathless and husky.

'You give me the right every time you look at me like that,' he said, tracing a pathway down the neckline of her top.

She felt her breasts tighten in anticipation. Her breathing stalled. Her heart stuttered like an old diesel engine inside her chest. She scrunched her eyes closed, fighting for strength of will. 'I'm not even looking at you, see?' she said.

He leaned in closer. She *felt* him. She felt his thighs brush against hers, and a wave of heat went through her like a knife through soft butter. She felt the sexy breeze of his breath against the skin of her neck. She breathed in the warm, male scent of him: the sweat, the musk, the complex cologne with its intriguing layers of citrus, spice and wood. The hairs on the back of her neck lifted one by one as his lips moved against her skin in a caressing nibble that shot an arrow of need straight to her core.

Bella made a little whimpering sound in her throat, a mixture of frustration and acquiescence. 'I don't want you,' she said.

'I know you don't,' he said, brushing his lips against hers in a teasing touch and lift off caress.

'I hate you,' she said, but the words somehow lacked conviction.

'I know you do,' he said and sucked softly on her lower lip until her legs threatened to fold beneath her.

Bella grasped his head between her hands, seeking his mouth in blind passion. The hot press of his mouth on hers detonated her senses and sent them into a fiery tailspin. She pushed her body against his, hungry for him in a way she had never thought possible. She ached for his possession, an urgent pulsing ache that was centred at the feminine heart of her.

He gripped her hips and ground against her shamelessly as his mouth worked its masterful magic on hers. It was so raw and primal. She felt the hot, hard heat of him throbbing against her stomach. It awoke every earthy sense in her body.

His hands moved from her hips to tug at her clothes. Her senses shrieked in rapturous delight at the rough urgency. He had her sweater pulled up, her top out of her skirt and her bra undone before she could find the fastener on his jeans. The wintry air danced over her flesh, but before she could shiver, his calloused hands moved over her naked breasts, making every nerve twitch in response. Her nipples tightened as he rolled his thumb over them, her spine turning to liquid as he brought his mouth over each one in turn. She closed her eyes and gave herself up to the pleasure of feeling his rough, stubbly face moving over her soft skin.

His mouth came back to hers just as she undid his jeans. He grunted with approval as she finally freed him. The hot, silky length of him filled her hand. Her heart raced as she thought of him moving inside her. She had never been so lust-driven in her life. Every other sexual encounter paled to insignificance. No one had ever made her feel so alive and in tune with her senses. Her skin was super-sensitive to his touch, to the stroke and glide of his hands, to the hot, moist possession of his mouth.

He lifted up her skirt and ruthlessly ripped her knickers and tights down to her knees. Her mouth was still jammed on his, her tongue duelling with his in a battle that was not just about strength of wills but about mutual need.

He played her with his fingers, gently at first, exploring her in intimate detail, before upping the pace. She was swept up in the moment, unable to stop the sensations that ricocheted through her like a speeding bullet. She cried out as her body shuddered and shook against his fingers, her breath coming in startled gasps.

She sagged against him when it was over, shocked at how completely he had unravelled her.

Shocked and shamed.

She stiffened and pushed back from him, grabbing at her tights. 'Oh, dear God...'

His expression was inscrutable. 'We can finish this indoors,' he said, zipping up his jeans. 'I haven't got a condom in my tool belt.'

Bella felt anger shoot through her like a powerful, galvanising drug. This was all a game to him. He had no feelings for her. All he felt was lust. He had 'serviced' her to prove a point. He wanted to reduce her to a shameless hussy who was driven by physical desires instead of intellect and morality.

'You did that deliberately, didn't you?' she asked, shooting him a contemptuous glare as she tried to fix her disordered clothes. 'You seduced me like a common little trollop to prove a point.'

'I was right,' he said with a glinting look. 'You went off like a bomb.'

Bella swung her hand through the air and landed a stinging slap on his cheek. He barely flinched but her hand felt as if the bones had splintered. 'You…you *bastard*,' she said, cradling her hand to numb the jarring pain.

The silence pulsated with tension.

Bella suddenly wondered if he would hit her back. His face was a marble mask, his eyes soulless. Her gaze went to his hands; they were clenched tightly by his sides. Fear was like a cold, hard hand on the back of her neck. She stood rooted to the spot, staring at him with wide, uncertain eyes.

He slowly released a breath and unlocked his hands. 'Is that really the sort of man you think I am?' he asked.

She licked her paper-dry lips. 'I shouldn't have slapped you… I'm sorry…'

He picked up the ladder and tucked it under one arm. 'Apology accepted,' he said and strode away until he disappeared from sight.

CHAPTER SEVEN

EDOARDO sat behind the mahogany desk in the study and looked sightlessly at the figures in front of him on his computer screen. Work was usually the panacea for all ills but he couldn't get his brain to focus. All he could think about was the feel of Bella in his arms. His body still throbbed with desire. It was like a banked-down fire deep inside him. Just one spark of her gaze and he was alight again.

He had made her confront her desire for him but it had come at a price. The look on her face, the shadow of fear in her brown eyes as she had stood there, made his stomach churn. He had seen that look in his mother's eyes before his stepfather had raised his hand in one of his drunken rages. Even after all these years he could still hear the sound of that clenched fist landing on his mother's face or body.

He pushed back from the desk, stood up and wandered over to the window. The weather forecast had predicted a heavy fall of snow overnight. He could see the clouds gathering in brooding clusters on the horizon.

They reminded him of his mood.

Fergus got up from the rug with a tired sigh and made his way creakily to the door. Edoardo opened it for him just as Bella was walking past. She gave him a startled look and stepped backwards, one of her hands going to her milky throat. 'You scared me,' she said.

'That seems to be a habit of mine just lately,' he said.

Her eyes fell away from his. 'I know you're not like...that,' she said in a quiet voice.

'So you feel safe with me, do you, Bella?' he asked.

She slowly brought her toffee-brown eyes to his. 'Of course I do...'

'You don't sound very sure about that.'

Her teeth tugged at her lower lip for a moment. 'I know you would never physically hurt me,' she said.

'I sense a "but" lurking somewhere in that statement.'

She let out a wobbly little breath. 'This thing between us…it has to stop. It has to stop before it gets complicated.'

He slanted her a cynical smile. 'It's already complicated, Bella,' he said. 'Your father made it a hundred times more so by putting me in charge of your life.'

Her gaze appealed to his. 'You could always quit the guardianship. You'd be free of me and I'd be free of you. It's a win-win for both of us.'

'Not going to happen, princess,' he said. 'I made a promise to your father. He trusted me to keep you out of trouble. He worked damn hard to get where he got. I'm not going to stand by and see some gold-digging gigolo waltz into your life and take everything.'

'Why do you think I'm gullible enough to let something like that happen?' she asked with a frown.

'You're too trusting,' Edoardo said. 'You're so desperate for approval and acceptance you can't see the difference between genuine friendship and exploitation.'

She flashed him a glare. 'I have lots and lots of genuine friends. Not one of them exploits me.'

He cocked a brow. 'How much rent do you charge those four girls who share your house?'

She pressed her lips together without answering, her cheeks turning rosy red.

'Nothing, right?' he said. 'You're a fool, Bella. They're using you, and you can't or won't see it.'

'You know nothing about my friends,' she said. 'So I help them out with a place to stay— what of it? They help me in turn.'

'How?' he asked with a curl of his lip. 'Let me guess: they help you spend your allowance on useless fripperies each month.'

Her eyes gave an annoyed little roll. 'I don't have to explain my personal expenses to you.'

'For God's sake, Bella, you went through fifteen thousand pounds in the last couple of months,' he said. 'You can't keep spending like that. You have to take responsibility for yourself. I'm not going to be around to keep you on track for ever.'

She sent him a caustic look. 'I can keep myself on track. I don't need you.'

'You *do* need me,' he said. 'And you've got me for another year, so you'd better get used to it.'

'What's the point of stringing this crazy guardianship thing out for another year?' she asked. 'You want to be free of me just as much as I want to be free of you. Anyway, once I get married to Julian, you'll have to relinquish your hold over me.'

'You're not getting married until you're twenty-five,' he said. 'Not while I have anything to do with it.'

She clenched her hands by her sides, anger in

every rigid line of her body. 'Is that why you've been busily trying to seduce me any chance you could?' she asked.

He returned her fiery look with cool ease. 'Are you going to tell your God-fearing boyfriend that you've slept with me?'

Her eyes turned to flint. 'I have *not* slept with you.'

'Are you going to tell him you had an orgasm with me, then?' he asked.

Her cheeks bloomed with colour again. 'I didn't have any such thing *with* you. You didn't… you know…' She whooshed out a little breath and shifted her eyes from his. 'We didn't go that far.'

'You probably won't have to tell him.'

Her eyes flew back to his. 'What do you mean?'

'He'll know as soon as he sees you,' Edoardo said. 'You won't be able to hide it, especially if he sees you interact with me.'

She clamped her lips together as if she was

struggling to keep back a retort. She released them after a moment. 'I can't think of any situation or event where you and Julian would be present at the same time.'

'So you're not going to invite me to your wedding?' he asked.

She gave him a pointed look. 'Would you come if I did?'

Edoardo considered her question for a moment. Over the years his mind had occasionally drifted to the day when she would walk down the aisle to some man standing at the altar. He had no doubt she would make a beautiful bride. She would love being the centre of attention; it would be her chance to be a princess for the day.

But he hadn't planned on being there to see it.

'Weddings are not really my thing,' he said.

'Have you ever been to one?'

'Two, a few years ago,' he said. 'They're both divorced now.'

She folded her arms across her middle. 'Not

all marriages end up on the rocks,' she said. 'Many couples spend a lifetime together.'

'Good for them.'

She frowned at him. 'You don't believe love can last that long?'

'I think people get love and lust confused,' he said. 'Lust is a transient thing. It burns itself out after a while. Love, on the other hand, is something that grows over time, given the right conditions.'

'I thought you didn't believe in love,' she said.

'Just because I haven't been in love myself doesn't mean it doesn't exist,' he said. 'I can see it works for some people.'

'But you don't think I'm in love, do you?'

'I think you want to *be* loved,' he said. 'It's understandable, given that your father's gone and your mother has always been too selfish to love you properly.'

Her teeth snagged her bottom lip again. 'You're making me out to sound tragic.'

Edoardo studied her for a moment. 'Don't

throw your life away on someone who doesn't love you for the right reasons, Bella,' he said.

'Julian does love me for the right reasons,' she said. 'He's the first man I've met who hasn't pressured me to sleep with them. Doesn't that say something?'

'Is he gay?'

She gave him a look. 'Of course he's not gay. He has principles; standards. Self-control.'

'The man is a saint,' Edoardo said. 'I can't be in the same room as you without wanting to rip the clothes off your body and ravish you.'

Her eyes flitted away from his, her cheeks firing up yet again. 'You shouldn't say things like that,' she said.

'Why not?'

'You know why not.'

'You don't believe in speaking the truth?' he asked.

'Some things are better left unsaid.'

Edoardo came over to her and slowly lifted

her chin with the end of his index finger. 'What are you so afraid of?' he asked.

She moistened her lips with a nervous dart of her tongue. 'I'm not afraid of anything.'

'You're afraid of being out of control,' he said. 'I make you feel out of control, don't I, Bella? I'm not like all those simpering boyfriends you surround yourself with. You can control them, but you can't control me. You can't even control yourself when you're with me. It scares you that I have so much power over you.'

She gave him a glittering glare. 'You don't have any power over me.'

He arched a brow as he trailed a finger over her bottom lip. 'Don't I?' he asked.

Her lip trembled under his touch before she wrenched herself out of his reach. 'You want to wreck my life, don't you?' she asked, eyes flashing. 'You want to cause trouble for me because you've always resented me for being born to wealth while you were born to nothing. You think by dragging me down to your level it will somehow even the score. Well, it won't. You will always be a reject who landed on his feet.'

Her taunting words rang in the silence.

'Feel better now you've got that off your chest?' Edoardo asked.

She put up her chin, her brown eyes still glittering with defiance. 'I'm leaving,' she said. 'I'm not staying another minute here with you.'

'Good luck with that,' he said. 'It's been snowing like a blizzard for the last hour. You won't get as far as the end of the driveway.'

'We'll see about that,' she said and flounced out.

'Damn it.' Bella slammed her hands on the steering wheel in frustration. She had been so determined to prove Edoardo wrong. And she had almost done it, too. She *had* got further than the end of the driveway. She had made it to the road before her car had slipped sideways and become bogged up to the windows in a snowdrift. But now she was out of sight of the manor and, with the snow blocking the road for as far as she could see in either direction, she could be stuck here for hours. It was freezing cold in spite of the heater in her car. She knew she couldn't leave the engine running for too long without flattening the battery. She could call for roadside help, which might take hours to get here. Or she could call Edoardo.

She rummaged for her mobile in her bag on the seat beside her. She held it in her hand, looking at the screen for a long moment where she had pulled up Edoardo's number. As much as it pained her to admit defeat, she pressed the call button.

'Do you want me to come get you?' he asked without preamble.

Bella silently ground her teeth. 'If it's not too much trouble.'

'Stay in the car.'

She glanced at the wall of snow that had fallen against both of her doors. 'I can't get out even if I wanted to,' she said.

While she was waiting for Edoardo to come, her phone rang. Bella glanced at the caller ID and suppressed a groan. Her mother only ever called her when she wanted something, usually money. 'Mum,' she said. 'How are things?'

'Bella, I need to talk to you,' Claudia said. 'I'm in a bit of a fix financially. Have you got a moment to talk?'

Bella looked at the snow-covered landscape surrounding her little capsule of a car. 'All the time in the world,' she said with a jaded sigh. 'How much do you need?'

'Just a few thousand to tide me over,' Claudia said. 'I've decided to leave José. Things haven't been working out. I'm in London for a few days. I thought it'd be nice if we spent some time to-gether—hang out a bit, you know? Go shop-ping, do girly things.'

'I'm not in London right now,' Bella said.

'Where are you?'

'I'm…um, out of town.'

'Where out of town?' Claudia asked.

Bella drew in a little breath and carefully released it. Would it hurt to tell her mother where she was? Maybe if she were a little more open with her, Claudia would start acting more like a mother towards her. She longed to have someone to talk to who would understand. She was tired of feeling so isolated and alone. 'I'm at Haverton Manor.'

'With...with *Edoardo*?'

'Yes... Well, not *with* him as such,' Bella said. 'I hardly see him. He does his thing. I do mine. He's—'

'I suppose he's told you a heap of lies about me, has he?' Claudia said. 'Your father was a sentimental fool to let him take control of your affairs. How do you know if he's ripping you off or not? He could be selling off your assets behind your back and you wouldn't know a thing about it.'

'He's not ripping me off,' Bella said. 'He's managing everything brilliantly.'

'How can you possibly trust him to do the

right thing by you?' Claudia asked. 'Don't forget he would've gone to prison if it hadn't been for your father vouching for him. He's got bad blood.'

'I don't think you should judge someone on where or how they grew up,' Bella said. 'He had a difficult start in life. He was an orphan at the age of five. I think it's amazing how well he's done, given how hard things were for him.'

'Goodness me,' Claudia said. 'This is a turn up for the books, isn't it?'

Bella frowned. 'What do you mean?'

'You springing to Edoardo's defence,' Claudia said. 'You sound positively chummy with him. What's going on?'

'Nothing.' Bella could have kicked herself for answering so quickly. *Too quickly.*

She could almost see her mother's snide smile. 'You've slept with him, haven't you?'

'What on earth makes you think that?' Bella said, injecting her tone with as much disdain as she could. 'You know how much we've always hated each other.'

'Hate doesn't stop people having sex with each other,' Claudia said. 'Some of the best sex I've had was with men I positively loathed.'

Bella hadn't planned on telling Claudia about her engagement until it was official, but she would do almost anything to avoid an account of her mother's lurid and colourful sex life. 'I'm getting engaged,' she said.

'Engaged?' Claudia gasped. 'Oh, dear God, not to Edoardo?'

Bella frowned as she tried to imagine Edoardo putting a ring on her finger—or any woman's finger, when it came to that. She couldn't quite see it. He would never be one to declare his feelings if he had any. He would never admit to needing someone.

He certainly would *never* admit to needing *her*.

He wanted her, but that was different. He didn't need her in an emotional sense. He didn't need anyone. He was like a wolf that had separated himself from the pack. No one would ever see what he felt on the inside. 'No, not to Edoardo,' she said. 'To Julian Bellamy.'

'Have I met him?'

'No, we've only been dating for three months.'

'Is he rich?'

'That has nothing to do with anything,' Bella said. 'I love him.'

'When did you *not* love a boyfriend?' Claudia asked. 'You fall in and out of love all the time. You've been doing it since you were thirteen. What if he's only after your money?'

Bella rolled her eyes. 'You sound just like Edoardo.'

'Yes, well, he might not be from the right side of the tracks but he's certainly street smart,' Claudia said. 'Your father wouldn't have a bad word said about him. I think he secretly hoped you would make a match of it with him.'

'What?' Bella asked, her stomach doing a little free fall. 'With Edoardo?'

'Why else would he have written his will the way he did?' Claudia asked. 'I bet he put Edoardo in control so you would have to see him regularly. He was hoping you'd fall in love with each other over time.'

'I am *not* going to fall in love with Edoardo,' Bella said.

'You'd be the icing on the cake for a man like him,' Claudia continued. 'It would make his rags-to-riches tale complete, wouldn't it? The well-born trophy bride to produce some blue-blooded heirs to dilute the bad blood flowing in his veins.'

Bella felt a strange tingle deep in the pit of her belly when she thought of her body swelling with Edoardo's child. She put a shaky hand over her abdomen, trying to quell the sensation. 'Mum, I have to go,' she said. 'I'll send you some money as soon as I can. I'm…in the middle of something right now.'

'I suppose you'll have to ask Edoardo for permission,' Claudia said sourly. 'Don't let him come between us, Bella. I'm your mother. Don't ever forget that.'

'I won't,' Bella said, thinking of the day, all those years ago, when her mother had left with her lover without even bothering to wave good-bye.

Edoardo found Bella almost buried in a ditch fifty metres from the front gate to the manor. She wound down the window as he stepped off the tractor. 'If you're going to say I told you so, then please don't waste your breath,' she said.

'You don't do things by halves, do you?' he asked.

'Can you get me out?'

'Sure,' he said. 'Stay in the car and keep the wheels straight while I tow you out.'

She sat and glowered at him from behind the steering wheel as he hitched the towrope to the bumper bar. He towed the car out, and once it was out of the ditch, he got her to join him on the tractor for the journey back to the house.

'Are you warm enough?' he asked as he made room for her beside him on the seat. 'You can have my jacket.'

'I'm f-fine,' she said through chattering teeth.

He shrugged himself out of his jacket and wrapped it around her slim shoulders. 'You don't have to fight me just for the heck of it, Bella,' he said.

She bit her lip and looked away. 'It's a habit, I guess.'

'Habits can be broken.'

Edoardo drove the tractor with the car towed behind all the way back to the manor. The snow kept falling but even more heavily now. It cloaked everything as far as the eye could see in a thick white blanket.

The air was tight with cold.

Every breath he or Bella exhaled came out in a foggy mist in front of their faces. He glanced at her and saw her huddled inside his coat, her hands gripping the edges together across her chest. She looked small, defenceless and vulnerable. 'Hey,' he said gently, bumping her shoulder with his.

She blinked and looked at him. 'Sorry, did you say something?'

'Penny for them.'

'Pardon?'

'Your thoughts,' he said.

'Oh…'

'What's wrong?' he asked.

'Nothing.' She looked away again and huddled further into his jacket.

Edoardo brought the tractor to a stop and helped her down. She hesitated before she placed her hand in his. 'You're freezing,' he said, keeping her hand within the shelter of his.

'I forgot to bring my gloves,' she said.

He released her hand. 'Go inside,' he said. 'I'll sort your car out. Go get warm. I'll be in in a minute.'

'Edoardo?'

He straightened from where he was untying

the towrope from the bumper bar and looked at her. 'Yes?'

She chewed at her lower lip for a moment. 'I need some extra money,' she said. 'Would you be able to transfer five thousand into my account?'

He frowned. 'You don't have a gambling problem, do you?'

Her eyes widened in affront. 'Of course not!'

'What do you want it for?'

Her expression became haughty. 'I don't see why I have to tell you what I spend *my* money on,' she said.

'You do while I'm still in control of it,' he said.

'My mother thinks you're skimming off the profits to fund your own nest egg,' she said with a hard little look.

'And what do you think, Bella?' he asked. 'Do you think I'd stoop so low as to betray the trust your father placed in me?'

She turned to go to the house. 'I need the money as soon as possible.'

'For your mother, I presume?'

Her back stiffened, and after a tiny pause she turned back around to face him. 'If it was your mother, what would you do?' she asked.

'You're not helping her by propping her up all the time,' he said. 'She's become dependent on you. You'll have to wean her off or she'll eventually drain you dry. It's one of the reasons your father orchestrated things the way he did. He knew you would be too soft and generous. At least I can say no when it needs to be said.'

'Did she ask you for money when she came the other day?'

'Amongst other things.'

Her brows moved together. 'What other things?'

'I'm not going to badmouth your mother to you,' he said. 'Suffice to say I'm not her favourite person in the world.'

She nibbled at her lower lip. 'I'm sorry if she offended you.'

'I've got a thick skin,' he said. 'Now, go inside before yours is frozen solid.'

She met his gaze again. 'I didn't mean what I said earlier, you know. I think you're one of the most decent men I've ever met.'

'The cold has got to you, hasn't it?' Edoardo said with a teasing half-smile.

Her gaze fell away from his and he rolled up the towrope as he watched her walk towards the manor, her slim figure still encased in his jacket. It was so big on her it almost came to her knees. She looked like a child who had been playing in the dress-up box. He felt a funny tug inside his chest, as if a tiny stitch was being pulled against his heart.

Once the door had closed behind her, he let out a breath he hadn't realised he had been holding. 'Don't even go there,' he muttered under his breath and strode towards the barn.

CHAPTER EIGHT

EDOARDO came into the kitchen an hour later to find Bella poring over a cookbook that belonged to Mrs Baker. She had an apron on over her clothes and there was a swipe of flour across her left cheek. She looked up as he came in. 'I hope you don't mind, but I'm cooking dinner,' she said. 'I thought I should start to pull my weight around here since I can't leave right now.'

He hitched up one brow. 'Can you cook?'

She gave him a quelling look. 'I've been taking lessons from one of my flatmates,' she said. 'She's a sous chef in a restaurant in Soho.'

'The one your ex-boyfriend owned?'

She gave a little sigh as she looked at the ingredients in front of her. 'I only went out with him a couple of times,' she said. 'The press made it out to be much more than it was. They always do that.'

'I guess everyone wants to know what Britain's most eligible girl is up to,' he said.

'I sometimes wish I didn't come from such a wealthy background,' she said with a little frown.

Edoardo leaned against the counter. 'You don't mean that, surely?' he said. 'You lap it up. You always have. You wouldn't know what to do with yourself if you didn't have loads of money.'

'My friends' mothers give *them* money or buy them stuff or take them shopping,' she said, still frowning. 'I'm tired of feeling responsible for my mother's bills.'

'You gave her the money?'

'Yes, and she hasn't even sent a text or called me to thank me.' She let out a dispirited sigh. 'She's probably spent it all by now.'

'I've been thinking about what I said earlier,'

he said. 'It's really none of my business who you give your money to. She's your mother. I guess you can't turn your back on her.'

After a little silence she looked up at him with those big brown eyes of hers. 'I wish I could be sure people liked me for *me*. How can I know if they like me because of who I am as a person? I don't even know if my mother loves me or simply sees me as a meal ticket.'

He reached forwards to brush the flour off her cheek with the end of his index finger. 'Sorting out the friends from the hangers-on is always a challenge, even for a person without wealth. You just have to trust your gut feeling, I suppose.'

Her shoulders went down as she sighed again. 'I think what you said before was right: I want to be loved so much that it clouds my judgement.'

'It's not wrong to want to be loved,' he said. 'We wouldn't be human if we didn't.'

She looked up at him again, her eyes soft and luminous. 'Do you want to be loved?'

Edoardo gave an off-hand shrug. Loving was something he didn't do any more. He suspected he had forgotten how. He certainly wasn't booking in any time soon for a refresher course either. 'I can take it or leave it.'

A little frown creased her forehead. 'You can't really mean that,' she said. 'You just don't want to be let down again or abandoned.'

He curled his lip, threatened by how close to the truth she was. He refused to let anyone close to him. Godfrey had been an exception, but it had taken years, and even then he hadn't told him everything about his past. 'Got me all figured out, have you, Bella?'

'I think you push people away because you're frightened of becoming too attached,' she said. 'You like to be in total control of your life. If you had feelings for someone else, they could take advantage of you. They could leave you just like your parents did.'

Edoardo felt a ridge of steel ripple through his jaw until his teeth were locked so tightly together he wondered if he'd be left with nothing but powder.

He thought of the first home he had been sent to after the authorities had stepped in when he'd been ten years old. He had already had five years of his stepfather's capricious and cruel treatment. Five years of living in dread, quaking with fear night and day in case things turned nasty.

The hands that had fed and clothed him, and at times even been kind to him, could turn within a blink of an eye into vicious weapons. It didn't matter how well-behaved he was. Sometimes the anticipation of the brutality was so torturous he would deliberately play up just to get it over with. But even then he could never prepare himself. He'd had no way of knowing when his stepfather would strike. His body had run solely on adrenalin. The 'flight or fight' mode had been jammed on.

He hadn't stood a hope of settling in anywhere.

Looking back now, he could see the foster parents he had been sent to had done their best. Some had been better than others; they had tried to offer him shelter and support but he had sabotaged their every attempt to get close to him. Then Godfrey Haverton had taken him in and, in his quiet and unobtrusive way, shown him that it was up to him to make something of his life. Under Godfrey's steady but sure tutelage, he had learned how to become a man, a man with self-control and self-respect—a man who was the agent of his own destiny, not at the mercy of others.

But he wasn't going to parade his past to Bella, of all people. He had locked it away and it was staying there.

'You don't know what the hell you're talking about,' he said.

'I think I do,' she said in a quiet and assured voice that was far more threatening than if she had shouted the words at him. 'I think you want what everyone else wants. But deep down you feel you don't deserve it.'

He gave her a mocking look. 'Did you read that in a self-help book, or is it something you just made up on the spot?'

She drew in a breath and slowly released it. 'I didn't read it anywhere,' she said. 'I just sense it—the same way my father sensed it. I think he understood you from the word go. He didn't push you or force affection on you. He waited for you to come to him when you trusted him enough to do so.'

Edoardo gave a disparaging laugh but the sound grated even on his own ears. 'You're making me sound like an ill-treated dog,' he said.

Her eyes meshed with his, soft and yet all-seeing—*knowing*.

The silence stretched and stretched.

He felt every beat of it like a hammer blow inside his head.

'What happened to you, Edoardo?' she asked.

The memories tapped him on the shoulder with their long, craggy fingers: *Come here,* they taunted. *Remember the time he hit you with the belt until you were bleeding? Remember the icy-cold showers? Remember the gnawing hunger? Remember the raging thirst?*

He pushed them away but one more crept up behind him and caught him off-guard.

Remember the cigarettes?

'Stop it, Bella,' he said tightly. 'I have no interest in dredging up stuff I've forgotten long ago.'

'You haven't forgotten it, though, have you?' she asked.

He clenched and unclenched his fists, his stomach feeling as though a crosscut saw was working its way through it. He felt the pain in his back. It had happened so long ago but he could still remember the searing pain and the helplessness. Oh, dear Lord, how he had hated the helplessness. Sweat broke out on his upper lip. He could feel it beading between his shoulder blades as well. His head throbbed with the memories, all of them jostling for their starring moment centre-stage.

'Edoardo?' Bella's hand touched him on the arm. 'Are you all right?'

Edoardo looked down at her. She was standing so close he could smell her shampoo as well as her perfume. Her eyes were full of concern, her soft mouth slightly open. He could hear her breath going in and out in soft little gusts.

His mobile phone pinged with the sound of an in-coming text, and the memories scuttled back to the shadows like sly, secretive rats running from the light of an opened door.

He let out a slowly measured breath. 'I know you mean well, Bella, but there are some things that are just best forgotten,' he said. 'My childhood is one of them.'

She stepped back from him, her hand falling back by her side. 'If ever you want to talk about it...'

'Thanks, but no,' he said and, briefly checking his phone, added, 'Look, I won't be in for dinner after all.'

Her expression clouded. 'You're going out in this weather?'

'Rebecca Gladstone needs a hand with something,' he said. 'I'm not sure how long I'll be.'

She screwed up her mouth, her eyes losing their softness to become glittery and diamond-hard. 'What does she need a hand with?' she asked. 'Turning back the sheets on her bed?'

'Green doesn't suit you, Bella.'

Her brows jammed together. 'I'm not jealous,' she said. 'I just think it's disgusting to lead someone on when you have no intention of taking their feelings seriously.'

'You're a fine one to talk,' he said.

'What's that supposed to mean?'

'While your intended fiancé is out of sight, you've been up to all sorts of mischief, haven't you?'

She coloured up and glowered at him at the same time. 'At least I'm not messing with your feelings,' she said. 'You don't have any, or at least certainly not for me.'

'Does that annoy you, Bella?' he asked. 'That I haven't prostrated myself before you like all your other suitors, declaring my undying love for you at every available opportunity?'

She gave him a flinty look. 'I wouldn't believe you if you did.'

Edoardo gave a little rumble of laughter. 'No, you wouldn't, would you? You know me too well for that. I might want you like the very devil, but I don't love you. That stings a bit, doesn't it?'

'It doesn't bother me one little bit,' she said with a pert hitch of her chin. 'I have no feelings for you either.'

'Other than lust.'

Her cheeks pooled with colour. 'At least that is something I can control,' she said.

'Can you?' he asked, taking her chin between his finger and thumb, holding her gaze steady. 'Can you really?'

Her throat rose and fell, and her eyes flickered. 'Why don't you try me and see?'

He was sorely tempted. He felt the urge rising in him like a flash flood. Blood pumped and poured. His need for her was a hungry beast inside him, rampaging through his body until he was almost shaking with it.

But instead he dropped his hand from her face and stepped away. 'Maybe some other time,' he said.

For a nanosecond he thought her expression showed disappointment, but she quickly masked it. 'There's not going to be another time,' she said. 'As soon as this snow melts, I'm out of here.'

'What if it doesn't melt for another week?' he asked as he shouldered open the door.

She set her mouth grimly. 'Then I'll go out there with a hair dryer and melt it myself.'

Bella slept fitfully until about two in the morning. She got up and looked out of the window.

The snow was still falling but not as heavily now. It looked like a winter fairyland outside. It was a scene she was going to miss dreadfully when she left Haverton Manor for the final time. She tried to imagine how it would be once the guardianship period was over. There would be no reason to see Edoardo again. No more twice-yearly meetings. No more monthly phone calls, texts or emails. He would go his way and she would go hers.

They would never have to see or speak to each other ever again.

She turned from the window with a frown. She had to stop thinking about him. She had to stop wondering why he was the enigma he was. What had put that hard cynicism in his eyes? What had made him so self-sufficient that nothing or no one touched his heart?

She couldn't stop thinking of him as a little five-year-old orphan. Who had looked after him? Comforted him? Who had nurtured him? Who had loved him? Had anyone?

For all these years she had thought of him as a rebel who didn't fit in anywhere, who didn't *want* to fit in anywhere. But what if his childhood had made him that way? What would it take to unlock the guard he had on his heart?

Would he ever come to a point in his life where possessions and financial security were no longer enough? Would he crave the connection he had been pushing away for most of his life?

Bella went downstairs in search of a hot drink and was waiting for the milk to heat in the microwave when Edoardo came in. He was still dressed in the clothes he'd had on earlier and there were snowflakes in his hair.

'Waiting up for me, Bella?' he asked as he shrugged off his coat.

She gave him a scornful look. 'You must be joking.'

'Rebecca sends her regards,' he said and dusted the snow out of his hair with one hand.

Bella glared at him. 'You talked about me while you were…in *bed* together?'

'We weren't anywhere near a bed.'

'Please spare me the lurid details,' she said with a roll of her eyes.

'I was helping her with a horse that had injured itself on a neighbouring property,' he said. 'Do you remember the Atkinsons' place? The new owner has thoroughbreds. One of the brood mares cut her foreleg on some wire. Rebecca needed an extra pair of hands.'

'Oh…' She chewed at her lip for a moment.

'Rob Handley is the new owner,' he said. 'He's a bit shy but he's fine once you get to know him.'

Bella frowned at him. 'Why are you telling me this?'

He gave a shrug. 'Just thought you might like to let Rebecca know some time if you're talking to her. Rob got off to a bad start with her. She thinks he's arrogant. It's a shame, because he really likes her. They'd make a great couple.'

Bella cocked her head at him. 'Don't tell me you're a romantic at heart?'

'Not at all,' he said. 'A blind man could see those two belong together. They just need a little nudge in the right direction. You want to make me one of those?' He indicated the hot chocolate she had on the counter.

Bella made the drink and handed it to him. Her fingers touched his and a shockwave of heat ran up her arm. She quickly put her hand back down by her side. 'While we're on the subject of perfect couples, I'd like to firm up some plans for my wedding,' she said.

His eyes collided with hers. 'No.'

Her brows snapped together. 'Will you at least listen to me?'

'You're making a big mistake, Bella,' he said. 'Can't you see how foolish this is? Look at what's been going on between us. How can you think you'll be happy settling down with a man who you can go for weeks or months without making love to you?'

Bella glared at him. 'Not every man is a slave to his desires,' she said. 'Some men have self-control.'

'Yeah, well, let's see how much self-control he has after a year,' he said.

'I'm not waiting a year,' she said. 'I told you. I want to get married in June.'

'What is a year in terms of your whole life?' he said. 'Rushing into marriage can be disastrous for women, even in this enlightened day and age.'

'I'll sign a pre-nuptial agreement if that will ease your concern,' she said. 'I'm sure Julian won't mind. In fact he'll probably insist on it.'

'It's not just about the money,' he said. 'I don't believe you're in love with this guy. How can you be? Look at how you respond to me.'

Bella glared at him. 'That's *your* fault.'

'How is it my fault?'

'Because you've done nothing but try it on with me from the moment I arrived,' she said. 'You haven't touched me in years, not since that night when I was sixteen. Why now? Why now when I'm about to marry someone else?'

His jaw clenched tight as he put his mug down on the counter. 'You think I haven't wanted to touch you over the years?' he said. 'God damn it, Bella, are you blind? Of course I wanted to touch you. You were too young back then and you were half-tanked with alcohol. By the time I felt you were old enough, your father got sick. And then he died, and when he made me your guardian, that complicated things.' He raked a hand through his hair. 'If I'd known what your father had planned, I would've tried to talk him out of it.'

Bella frowned at him. 'I thought you cooked this up with him,' she said. 'Did you really know nothing about it?'

He sucked in a breath and released it audibly. 'I knew he was worried about how you would manage your wealth,' he said. 'He felt you would be easy pickings for someone who was after your money. He knew you had a soft heart.'

'I didn't show much of that soft heart when he needed it, did I?' she asked sadly.

He tipped up her chin and met her eyes. 'It wasn't all your fault, Bella,' he said. 'Your father could be very stubborn when he wanted to be. He pushed you away just as much as you pushed him away.'

'Like you do?'

He dropped his hand from her face. 'I'm nothing like your father.'

'Yes you are,' Bella said. 'That's why you got on so well. You were kindred spirits. He saw himself in you. I've never realised it until now. He had a rough start in life, too. His mother died when he was young; I think he was only about six or seven. He was sent to live with distant relatives because his father had to go away for work. He didn't like talking about it. It was like a wound he didn't want anyone else to see.'

'You've really missed your calling, haven't

you?' he said with a sneer of a smile. 'Just think, if you hadn't made a career out of doing lunch and shopping, you could've have been a psychologist.'

'Go on,' Bella said, glaring at him in irritation. 'Mock me. Make fun of me. That's what *you've* made a career out of, isn't it?'

He came up close and grabbed her chin between his finger and thumb. 'Let's see how good your psychologist's skills are, shall we?' he said. 'Why do you think you're rushing off to marry a man you barely know?'

Bella stared him down. 'I love him, that's why.'

'You're panicking, that's why,' he said. 'You've only got a year until a truckload of money lands in your lap. You're not sure how you're going to handle it, are you? You're worried that it will be too much to deal with on your own so you've latched on to the first reliable, steady person you think will be able to help you.'

'That's not true,' she said. 'I want to settle

down and have a family. I don't want to be on my own any more. I want to belong to someone.'

He pulled her up against him. 'You're frightened of the passion that's burning inside you,' he said. 'You're worried you're going to end up like your mother, flitting from shallow affair to shallow affair.'

Bella strained against his iron-strong hold. 'I'm nothing like my mother,' she protested. 'I'm not going to marry for lust. Lust doesn't come into it at all.'

'No, well, it can't, can it?' he said. 'Not when your lust is directed elsewhere.'

Bella felt the hot probe of his erection. She felt the need rising up in her like a giant, swamping wave. It overpowered her defences. How could she resist him when her body was programmed to respond to him and only him? 'I don't want to want you,' she said.

He fisted a hand in her hair, his mouth so close she could feel his breath on her lips. 'Do you think I want to want you?' he asked. 'I've fought it for as long as I can remember.'

It thrilled Bella to hear his gruff confession. For so long she had thought he felt nothing for her. His indifference had annoyed her so intensely, but all that time he had been fighting his attraction.

But what was the point in telling her now? *Why* was he telling her now?

'Don't you think you've left it a bit late to tell me?' she said. 'I'm about to announce my engagement.'

He brushed his mouth against hers, once, twice. 'Is it too late?' he asked.

Bella wasn't sure what he was asking. She licked her dry lips and looked at his mouth, that sensual, wicked mouth that could make her feel things she had no right to be feeling. She wanted to feel that mouth on hers again. She wanted to feel that mouth on her body, on her breasts, on her inner thighs, on the very heart of her desire. 'You don't love me,' she said, running a fingertip over his bottom lip, her soft skin catching on his evening stubble.

'You don't love me either,' he said. 'If you did, you wouldn't be promising to marry someone else, now, would you?'

She sent her fingertip over the contour of his upper lip this time. 'Would you want me to love you?' she asked.

'No,' he said. 'That's not what I want at all.'

She stilled the movement of her finger and looked up into his eyes, her heart beating double time at the smouldering look in his blue-green gaze. 'Then what do you want?' she asked.

He cupped her bottom with his hands, bringing her in close to the heated trajectory of his erection. 'Do you really need to ask that?' he said.

Bella felt her breath hitch in her chest as his head came down in slow motion towards hers. She had the chance to step away. She had the chance to say no. She had more than enough time to tell him she had no intention of making love with him.

But she didn't.

CHAPTER NINE

BELLA closed her eyes just as his mouth touched down on hers. It was one of those brush-and-release kisses that made her senses sing with delight. His tongue flickered against hers, cajoling hers into erotic play. She responded with a shiver of reaction that felt like champagne bubbles flowing beneath her skin.

He increased the pressure of his lips on hers, the taste-and-tease action of his tongue changing to a more determined thrust and retreat. The primal intent was unmistakable. It made her body hum with longing to feel him inside her, stroking, thrusting. She could already feel the dew of need between her thighs and that little clenching pulse pulling on her inner muscles.

She gave a soft whimper as he cupped the

back of her head as his tongue drove deep into her mouth, his pelvis rock-hard against hers. She was spinning with need, her hands flying all over him to find access to his skin. 'I want you,' she whispered breathlessly against his mouth. 'I know it's wrong, but I want you.'

'It's not wrong,' he said and ran his hands up under her jumper in search of her breasts. 'It's inevitable. It always has been.'

Bella gasped as his calloused hands caressed her. She worked at his shirt buttons, not even caring that one of them popped off and pinged to the floor. She pressed hot kisses to his neck and down his sternum, her hands going on ahead and working on the belt and fastener on his jeans.

He growled in male pleasure as she finally uncovered him. He was so thick and strong in her hand, silky smooth and already moist at the tip. 'Bedroom,' he said against her lips and swept her up in his arms.

'I'm too heavy,' she protested. 'You'll do your back in.'

'Don't be ridiculous,' he said. 'What sort of men have you been dating? You weigh next to nothing.' He shouldered open the door and carried her upstairs, stopping every now and again to torture her mouth with the heat and fire of his.

Bella was almost out of her head with need by the time they got to his bedroom. He laid her on the bed and came down over her, his mouth clamping down on hers. She ran her hands up under his loosened shirt, discovering the planes and contours of his back and shoulders. He was so lean and yet so muscular, his skin warm and dry to her touch. She could smell the hint of man beneath the intricate layers of his aftershave. It called out to the primal woman in her, in a language as old as time itself.

He leaned his weight on one arm as he ripped off his shirt and tossed it to the floor at the side of the bed. Bella shivered in anticipation as he started to remove her clothes. Her jumper went first, ending up on the floor. Her bra followed, but not before he had suckled each of her nipples through the lace. It was such an erotic thing to do, and the tickly barrier of the lace somehow made it all the more pleasurable.

He kissed his way down her stomach, dipping his tongue in the tiny pool of her belly button. She felt herself tensing as his fingers started to peel back the lace of her knickers.

'What's wrong?' he asked, stilling his hand. 'Am I going too fast?'

'No… It's just I haven't waxed recently.'

'Good,' he said. 'There's nothing I like more than a real woman.'

Bella held her breath as he gently tugged the lace down to uncover her. She saw the way his eyes darkened with desire. 'You're beautiful,' he said.

The sensation of his finger outlining her form was unbelievable. He explored her with his fingers, taking it gently, waiting for her to relax before he inserted a finger, then two. He withdrew his fingers and lowered his mouth to her, tasting her in a gentle sweep of his tongue. She breathed in sharply as the sensations took her by surprise. What if she made a fool of herself? It was too intimate. What if she didn't respond properly? She gasped and tried to pull away.

'Relax,' he soothed. 'Go with it. Don't tense up.'

'I'm not very good at this,' Bella said, biting down on her lower lip.

'This is about you, not me. It's your pleasure. You take all the time you need.'

She lay back as he continued stroking her softly, his fingers gentle and yet sure. He waited until she was totally at ease before he caressed her again with his tongue. He used slow, stroking movements, gauging her reaction, varying the pressure and speed until she felt the sensations ricocheting through her. They came in rolling waves that coursed through and over her, spinning her, tossing her, tumbling her, until she was gasping out loud. 'Oh, God,' she said in a rush. 'That was...unbelievable.'

He came back over her, brushing her hair back from her forehead with his hand, his eyes thoughtful as they studied hers. 'You're not very confident sexually, are you?' he said.

Bella lowered her gaze and stared at his Adam's apple. 'I'm not a virgin, if that's what you're asking. I've had sex heaps and heaps of times.'

His index finger tipped up her chin. 'How many partners have you had?'

She looked into his blue-green gaze. 'Five...'

He tilted his head. 'Five?'

She blew out a little breath. 'OK, six, if you count the first time, but I never do as it was a complete and utter disaster.'

'What happened?'

'It was that Christmas I stayed in town,' she said. 'I was determined to prove I was mature enough to have sex, contrary to what you had said that night when we kissed. I hate to say it, but you were right; I wasn't mature enough. It was over before it began. I ended up in tears and the guy left the party with someone else.'

He smoothed her hair again, his eyes holding hers in a sensual lock that made her insides quiver with longing. 'I want you,' he said. 'I wanted you then and I want you now.'

Bella locked her arms around his neck, her pelvis on fire where it was being probed by the heat of his. 'Make love to me,' she whispered.

He bent his head to her mouth, kissing her with drugging sensuality. Her spine melted like honey in a heatwave. His erection throbbed with primal urgency against her and she instinctively went in search of it, shaping him with her fingers, delighting in the deep guttural groan he made against her lips.

His mouth moved to her breasts, subjecting each one to a hot swirl of his tongue before suckling on her. Then, even more pleasurably, he trailed his tongue to the sensitive underside of each breast, making the nerves beneath her skin go haywire.

Bella writhed beneath him, desperate for that final possession. Her body was slick with want. 'Please…' she said.

He reached for a condom and handed it to her. 'You want to put it on me?'

Bella tore the packet with her teeth, took the condom out and carefully pulled it over him, caressing him as she went. He sucked in a breath, pushed her back down and came over her, his weight supported on his arms. He parted her gently, waiting for her to accept him before going further. She became impatient and lifted her hips towards his. He groaned again and surged into her with a long, thick thrust that sent a shiver down her spine.

He started to move, slowly at first, but then the pace picked up. Bella felt each delicious movement, the friction sending her senses reeling. Every tiny muscle in her body tensed as the pressure built. She could feel her body climbing, straining, crying and screaming out for release that was frustratingly just out of her reach.

He slipped a hand beneath her bottom and lifted her higher against him, his thrusts even more determined. 'Don't hold back, Bella,' he said. 'Let yourself go.'

His other hand went in search of the heart of her need, the tiny, swollen pearl of her clitoris that was so sensitive she could not hold back a gasp as the storm in her body erupted. She gripped him tightly, her teeth sinking into his shoulder as the tumultuous waves picked her up and tossed her into the abyss. Around and around she went, a burst of sensations like a thousand explosions inside her body.

Bella held him as he worked towards his own release, the thrusting motion of his body sending aftershocks of pleasure through hers. She stroked his back and shoulders, feeling the tight clench of his muscles as he pitched forward into oblivion. He groaned deeply and shuddered, his breath coming out in a harsh gasp against her neck.

She listened to the sound of his breathing in the aftermath, holding his totally relaxed body against hers. She didn't want to move. Her body was in such a blissful state of lassitude, every muscle felt like it had been set free. She was floating in a sea of ecstasy, in tune with her body in a way she had never been before.

'I don't want to move just yet,' he said against the sensitive skin below her earlobe.

'Nor me,' she said as she slid her hands over the taut curve of his buttocks.

He positioned himself above her by leaning on one of his forearms, and the other hand he used to trace a feather-light pathway over each of her eyebrows, her nose, her cheeks, her top lip and then her lower one. 'You were amazing,' he said. 'Truly amazing.'

Feeling a little out of her depth, Bella focused her gaze on his collarbone, tracking her fingertip back and forth along its ridge. 'It's never been like that for me before,' she said. 'I've never…you know…'

A frown moved through his eyes. 'You've never orgasmed during sex?' he asked.

'No,' she said. 'It's my fault, I know. I over-think everything and worry about stuff. I get myself in a state. I'm always kind of relieved when it's over.'

He cupped her face, his thumb stroking along her cheek in a slow caress. 'What stuff do you worry about?'

Bella rolled her lips together. 'The usual: my thighs, my stomach, my breasts.'

His frown was incredulous. 'Bella, you're beautiful. You're perfect. How can you possibly worry about things like that?' he asked.

'I know, it sounds so…so shallow,' she said.

'Not shallow,' he said. 'Just insecure.'

'Yep,' Bella said with a self-deprecating twist of her mouth.

His thumb paused in its stroking action, his blue-green gaze steady on hers. 'You have no need to be. You really don't. You're one of the most beautiful women I've ever met.'

She gave him a tremulous smile. 'Thank you.'

He brushed the pad of his thumb over her bottom lip. 'This thing between us...' He paused for a moment. 'I want it to continue.'

Bella's heart gave a little stumble. 'For how long?'

He studied her expression for another beat or two. 'I'm not one for putting a timeline on relationships,' he said. 'Let's just see how it goes, shall we?'

Bella felt reality slap her in the face. She knew exactly how it would go: he would have his fun and move on. He wasn't promising her anything—no emotion, no love, no future—just sex. Right from the start, all he had wanted to do was to stop her marrying before she was twenty-five. What better way than to temporarily distract her with the delights of his love-making? But how long would an affair between them continue? Even if it did continue for a few weeks, or even months, he wasn't going to offer her the things she yearned for most. 'Aren't you forgetting something?' she asked.

His brows came together. 'You're surely not still determined to go ahead with that ridiculous engagement?'

'Why wouldn't I?' she asked.

He lifted himself away and got off the bed, one of his hands raking a pathway through his hair. 'I'm offering you a relationship.'

'You're offering me a fling,' Bella said.

His cheek moved in and out as he clenched his teeth. 'That's all I can offer you,' he said.

'It's not enough for me,' she said, swinging her legs over the bed to collect her clothes. 'I don't want to live like my mother, going from fling to fling. I want to settle down.'

'How can you sell yourself so short?' he asked, capturing her arm to stop her moving past. 'You're setting yourself up for a passionless life. Why can't you see it?'

Bella tried to shake off his hold but he held her fast. 'I want a normal life.'

'What's normal about marrying a man you don't love?' he asked.

'I *do* love him,' she said.

He gave a mocking grunt. 'And yet you just had sex with me.'

'It was just sex,' she said. 'It's just a physical thing. It means nothing.'

'Do you really believe that?' he asked.

Bella wanted to believe it. She *needed* to believe it. 'I should never have slept with you,' she said. 'It was a mistake. I wasn't thinking.'

'No, maybe not, but you were feeling,' he said, pulling her closer, right up against his naked body. 'Like you're doing now. Can you feel what you do to me, Bella? What we do to each other?'

Bella could and it sent a wave of hot, pulsing longing through her. His erection was pressed against her thigh. She felt her feminine core tingling in anticipation, the nerve-endings still sensitised from their passionate coupling earlier.

His mouth came down and covered hers and in a heartbeat she was lost. Her arms snaked around him, holding him as close as she possibly could. She wanted to crawl inside his skin, to melt into him so that her body didn't ache with this maddeningly feverish want.

Her hands delved into his hair, her fingers threading through the thick black strands. She breathed in the scent of him, that erotic mix of his maleness with the delicate overlay of her perfume and body musk.

His hands slid down to the curve of her back and pressed her hard against him. Bella felt the potent power of him like an electric current through her body. All of her senses were screaming for his possession—it was a raw hunger that could not be satiated any other way.

She took him in her hand, stroking him, relishing the satiny feel of his skin, delighting in the iron-strong length of him. She loved hearing those deep, unmistakably male noises he made in the back of his throat—guttural groans that had a distinctly primal quality to them. She loved the way his mouth moved with such heated fervour on hers, the way his stubble was so sexily raspy on the soft skin of her face.

He used his teeth in playful little bites against her lips, tugging and releasing, tantalising her with that little hint of danger in the caress. She bit back with little nips that she followed up with gentle sweeps and flicks of her tongue.

He walked her backwards, thigh against thigh until the backs of her knees felt the bed. She tumbled backward, all legs and arms and red-hot need. He quickly applied a fresh condom and came down over her, his weight pinning her down, his mouth still locked on hers as his body speared hers in one deliciously vigorous thrust that made the breath hitch in her throat and her bones melt.

He set a fast pace that made shivers course down her spine and the fine hairs on the back of her neck dance and twitch in response. She felt the contraction of her muscles, all the sensitive nerves twanging as he rocked against her with passionate, heart-stopping urgency.

'You drive me insane, do you know that?' he said against her kiss-swollen mouth.

'Ditto,' Bella said, taking another nip at his lower lip.

He worked his way down her neck. 'Am I going too fast for you?'

She angled her head so he could get better access. 'Can you go faster?'

'I don't want to hurt you,' he said, pulling back his pace a bit. 'You're so tiny compared to me. I feel like I'm crushing you.'

'You're not,' she said, urging him on with little hip movements. 'You feel just right.'

He kissed her mouth again, lingeringly and tantalisingly. Bella writhed beneath him, her body so wired she felt like she was going to implode. He read her movements as if he had direct access to her thoughts and feelings. He slipped a hand between their bodies and found the swollen nub of nerve-endings that were all shrieking and clamouring for release.

It was a cataclysmic explosion of feeling. Her whole body quaked with it as if she had been caught in the epicentre of an earthquake. She couldn't stop from crying out, her breath coming out in jerky little gasps as the aftershocks shuddered through her.

She was still gasping as he came. She felt every powerful thrust as he emptied himself. She skated her hands down his back, holding him against her, wanting to prolong the deep connection of their bodies. There was something profoundly moving about his total loss of control. Was she deluding herself to think that what they had experienced together was different from anything else he had encountered with previous partners? Was it crazy of her to want to be something to him other than yet another sexual conquest?

Edoardo eased himself up on his forearms

to look at her. 'You're frowning,' he said as he brushed a flyaway strand of hair back off her face. 'I didn't hurt you, did I?'

'No, of course not,' Bella said, lowering her gaze.

He smoothed the little crease between her eyebrows with the pad of his finger. 'I know what you're thinking.'

She gave him a wry look. 'So you can read my mind as well as my body, can you?'

He searched her gaze for a moment. 'Don't beat yourself up for giving in to me,' he said. 'This was always going to happen—you and me in bed together.'

'Because you wanted to prove a point.'

'I'm not trying to prove anything,' he said, frowning a little. 'I just think you need to take a bit more time about your decision. You're panicking about your future; it's understandable. You're about to inherit a fortune. It's a lot of responsibility for someone so young. You're looking for someone to help share that responsibility—someone reliable. But I don't want you to make a mistake that you'll end up regretting for the rest of your life.'

'Would you approve of *anyone* I chose to marry?' she asked.

He held her gaze for a beat or two before he moved away to get off the bed. 'I'd better let Fergus out,' he said.

Bella frowned as she saw him reach for his trousers on the floor. 'What's that on your back?'

'It's nothing,' he said, shaking out the creases in his trousers and stepping into them. 'Just a couple of chicken-pox scars.'

She grabbed at the sheet and draped it around herself as she padded over to him. 'They look pretty big for chicken-pox scars,' she said, putting a hand on his arm to stall him. 'Let me see.'

'Leave it, Bella,' he said and shrugged off her hold.

Bella looked up into his inscrutable features. 'Why have you got those little white circles below your tan line?' she asked. 'There must be eight or ten at least.'

It was an aeon before he spoke. A battle seemed to be playing out on his face. She could see the shadows flickering in his eyes as each second passed. The column of his throat looked tight, as if he was having trouble swallowing. His jaw was tightly clenched; she could see the in-and-out movement of a tiny muscle in the centre of his cheek. 'They're burns,' he said.

'Burns?' She frowned. 'What sort of burns?'

'Cigarette burns.'

Bella's eyes flared in shock. 'Cigarette burns? But how did you…? Oh, dear God.' She clapped her hands against her mouth, too horrified even to say the words out loud.

'Clever, wasn't it?' Edoardo said with bitterness in each and every word. 'He was careful to put them where no one would see. He couldn't get away with blackening my eyes or leaving me visibly bruised. He didn't want anyone asking tricky questions.'

Bella felt tears sprouting in her eyes. Her chest ached with the thought of him as a little boy being brutally burnt. What other horrors had he endured? Was that why he never spoke of his past? Was it just too horrible to recall? 'Your stepfather abused you?' she asked.

His mouth flattened to a thin line of bitterness. 'Only physically,' he said. 'He did worse to my mother.' A muscle twitched in his jaw. 'He was an absolute bastard to her. I couldn't do a thing to protect her. He wore her down until she finally gave up on life. She took an overdose. I found her.'

Bella swallowed as she thought of how awful it must have been for him. To find his mother dead, the one person he thought he could rely on gone for ever, leaving him under the care of a madman. How dreadful for a young child to be exposed to such violence. He must have been so terrified, so lost and alone once his mother had died. 'I'm so sorry…' she said, blinking back tears. 'It must have been dreadful for you.

I can't bear to even think about it. How on earth did you survive it?'

'Save your tears,' he said with a brusqueness that was jarring. 'I don't need anyone's pity.'

Bella's stomach churned with anguish as the thoughts came crowding in: a small motherless child with no one but a violent stepfather to take care of him; no loving father to go to for protection; no grandparents or extended family.

No one.

No wonder he was so self-reliant. He'd had no one to rely on since he was a little boy. He trusted no one. He needed no one. He loved no one.

'How did you finally get away from him?' she asked.

'The authorities stepped in when I was ten,' he said. 'A teacher at school noticed I was unwell. I hadn't had food for a week. They sent a social worker around.'

Her bottom lip trembled as she struggled to control her emotions. 'I'm so sorry...'

'It's in the past,' he said. 'I want to leave it there.'

'But what about justice?' she asked. 'Did your stepfather get arrested for child abuse?'

'He fed the authorities the line that I was a difficult kid,' he said. 'He couldn't control me. I was a rebel—I had conduct disorder, or some such thing. The thing is, I didn't know how to behave. I *was* uncontrollable. At times I was like a wild animal. I had so much anger stored up inside, I caused trouble and mayhem wherever I went.'

'But it wasn't your fault,' Bella said. 'The odds were stacked against you. But my father saw through all that to who you are on the inside—to who you had the potential to be.'

'Your father saved my life,' he said. 'I was on the road to nowhere when he offered me a home.'

'I think you helped him just as much as he helped you,' Bella said. 'You took his mind off the divorce from my mother. Before that he was sliding into a deep depression. You gave him a new focus. He really did see you as a surrogate son.'

Edoardo let out a jagged sigh. 'I didn't tell him about my past,' he said. 'I know he would have liked me to. He was very patient. He never pressured me but I just didn't want to go there.'

'Did he ever see the scars on your back?' Bella asked.

'No, but other people have.'

'Other people, as in lovers?'

'Yes,' he said, placing his arms through his shirt. 'But you're the first who didn't buy the chicken-pox story.' He slowly did up the buttons, his eyes still trained on hers. 'I hope I don't have to tell you that I would rather this didn't go public. I've spent years of my life trying to forget.'

She frowned. 'How could you think I would even think to do such a thing?'

'It wouldn't be the first time a woman sought revenge when things didn't go her way,' he said.

'You have an appalling view of women,' she said.

He gave a whatever shrug. 'Just speaking as I find.'

Bella bit her lip and looked away. She was just one of many lovers he'd had. Tonight was nothing out of the ordinary. It had rocked her world completely but it was just another encounter for him.

'What's wrong?'

She wrapped her arms around her body. 'Nothing.'

He came over and placed his hands on the tops of her shoulders. Bella felt his warm hard body behind her. She ached to lean back and give herself up to the pleasure of being in his arms. But hadn't she already stepped too far over the boundaries? How was she going to get back to her neat, ordered life? Her body would always want him. It wasn't something she could turn off or on at will. She had made it a whole lot worse by experiencing the sensual delights of his love-making. How would she ever settle for anyone else after him?

'Contrary to what you might think, this was special tonight,' he said against her hair.

She turned in his arms and looked up into his blue-green eyes. 'Do you really mean that?' she asked.

He cupped her face in his hands, his thumbs moving back and forth in a caressing motion across her cheeks as his eyes made love with hers. 'Do you have to go back to London straight away?' he asked.

Bella felt her heart do a crazy little somersault. 'What are you saying?'

He brushed his mouth against hers. 'Stay with me for a few days.'

Bella thought of the danger of staying with him. So many dangers—not just the danger of someone finding out about their affair, but the danger of her falling in love with him. Wasn't she more than halfway there already?

She linked her arms around his neck and said against his already descending mouth, 'I'll stay.'

CHAPTER TEN

THE snow had long melted but Bella kept putting off returning to London. She was aware of the clock ticking on her time with Edoardo. By tacit agreement neither of them mentioned her upcoming engagement. Bella felt as if the girl who was about to become engaged to Julian Bellamy was someone else entirely—nothing to do with her. It was like living a parallel existence. She had compartmentalised her life in such a way as to have it all, or at least to have what she could while she could.

And Edoardo was what she wanted.

Since the night he had revealed his past to her, she had started to see him for the sensitive and strong, resilient man he was underneath his cynical façade. He was an intensely private person. She had never met a more private person. He loathed gossip. He didn't have time for idle chit-chat. He was a man with a strong work ethic; he didn't believe in people being handed things for free.

He made Bella see her privileged background quite differently. She didn't like admitting it, but she *had* taken so much for granted. She hadn't thought much about the sacrifices her father had made in order to provide her with an inheritance that was beyond the dreams of most people. She felt incredibly guilty for resenting that her father hadn't focused all of his attention on her. But Edoardo made her see that her father had been working to provide for her, not for himself. Her father had been stung badly by the divorce from her mother and had spent the rest of his life rebuilding his empire so Bella could have a secure future. Her father had not said the words, but he had shown it in his actions.

As the week was drawing to a close, Bella

went down to the village for supplies and was shocked to see a couple of journalists with cameras at the ready step out of a car as she came out of a shop. She put her head down and turned to go back the other way but within moments they were striding alongside her on the footpath.

'Tell us about your relationship with the reclusive Edoardo Silveri,' one journalist said as he followed her along the footpath. 'Is it true you are currently staying with him at Haverton Manor, the house that once was your family home?'

Bella put her head down and kept walking. She knew from experience it didn't matter what she said; they would twist it to make it sound like something else entirely.

'A local source told us Mr Silveri was a teenage rebel with a criminal past,' another journalist said as they came alongside. 'Would you like to comment on what it's like to be involved with a bad boy who made good?'

Bella swung her gaze to the pushy journalist. She could not bear to have Edoardo painted in such a way. 'He's not a bad boy,' she said. 'He's never been bad. It's the people who let him down and hurt him who are bad. They're the ones who should be exposed and brought to justice.'

'Word has it Mr Silveri would never have made it without considerable help from your father,' the first journalist said.

Bella turned to face them. 'That's not true,' she said. 'Edoardo was always going to make it in spite of his background. That's just the sort of person he is. He's strong and determined. My father saw those qualities in him and nurtured them. He would be very proud of the man Edoardo has become. Now, please leave me alone. I have nothing more to say.'

Bella pretended to do more shopping until she was sure she wasn't being followed before she drove back to Haverton Manor. She wondered if she should tell Edoardo about the paparazzi in the village but then decided against it. She didn't want anything to spoil the rest of the time they had together. It would all too soon draw to a close. She couldn't stay down here for ever, even though she longed to. But she couldn't settle for anything less than total commitment. If Edoardo didn't love her enough to want to spend the rest of his life with her, then she would have to walk away, even though it would break her heart to leave him.

Bella had only been back at the manor half an hour when she got another call from her mother. She answered it while she was making the bed up with fresh linen in Edoardo's room. 'Mum,' she said tucking the phone between her cheek and her neck as she straightened the covers. 'I was wondering when you were going to call.'

'Yes, well, I've been busy sorting out the mess José left me with,' Claudia said. 'Speaking of bills, can you lend me a couple more thousand?'

'*Lend?*'

'Don't use that tone with me, young lady,' Claudia said. 'I'm still your mother, you know.'

'You're always leaning on me to sort out your finances. Dad gave you a massive settlement after the divorce. What have you done with it all?'

'Oh, well, now, listen to you,' Claudia said in a la-de-da tone. 'You're a fine one to criticise. You haven't had to work for anything in your life.'

'I know that,' Bella said. 'But I'm going to work now. As soon as I get my inheritance, I'm going to set up a trust fund for an orphanage. In the meantime, I'm going to look for work as a volunteer. I want to make a difference in a child's life, just like Dad did with Edoardo.'

'Your father's little experiment certainly back-fired, didn't it?' Claudia said.

'I'm not even going to ask you what you mean by that,' Bella said.

'I called around at the house in Chelsea and the girls said you weren't home,' Claudia said. 'Don't tell me you're still holed up with Edoardo.'

'I'm coming back on Saturday,' Bella said. 'I'm meeting Julian at the airport.'

'What's he going to think when he hears you've spent the last week or so with another man?' Claudia asked.

Bella moved away from the bed as if that would put some distance between her and her conflicted feelings. 'Mum, I'm not going to go ahead with the engagement. I want to talk to Julian in person about it. I don't think it's fair to him to do it on the phone.'

Claudia gave a little scoffing noise. 'That thug has got under your skin, hasn't he?' she said. 'I knew he would. I told you what he's up to. He wants you for your pedigree. Nothing else.'

Bella's hand tightened on the phone. 'Edoardo is *not* a thug,' she said. 'He's a gentle and caring man. You don't know him. He's not what you think at all.'

'You've been sleeping with him, haven't you?' Claudia said.

'Mum, I don't want to have this conversation with you.'

'He only wants you for your money,' Claudia said. 'That's why he won't allow you to give me any. He wants it all to himself.'

'No, that's not true,' Bella said, springing to his defence with all the emotion she had tried for so long to keep under wraps. It came bubbling out of her like a drain that had finally been unblocked. 'He's not offering to marry me. He won't marry anyone. It's because of his past. He suffered terribly as a child. You have no idea of what he's been through. He's the most amazing person I've ever met. I won't have you or anyone say such horrible things about him.'

'You silly little fool,' Claudia said. 'I suppose you fancy yourself in love with him, do you?'

Bella looked out of the window to where Edoardo was coming back across the fields with Fergus. He looked up and smiled at her, raising his hand in a wave. She smiled and waved back, her heart feeling as if someone had pressed it between two book ends. 'I think I have always loved him,' she said, but her mother had already ended the call.

Edoardo was clearing the last of the snow from the driveway when Bella came out to him. She was dressed in a pom-pom hat and mittens and looked so adorably cute he felt as if someone had grabbed him inside his chest. She had a little frown on her face and he put the shovel to one side so he could gather her hands in his. 'Why the long face?' he asked.

She blew out a breath that misted in front of her face. 'Nothing…'

He pushed up her chin. 'Hey,' he said. 'You were smiling when I waved to you half an hour ago. What's happened?'

She chewed at her lower lip. 'I had a talk to my mother.'

'And?'

Her shoulders went down. 'I told her I'm not

going to prop her up any more. She didn't like hearing it. She hung up on me.'

Edoardo gathered her close. 'You did the right thing,' he said. 'For too long you've been the parent in that relationship.'

She looked up at him with those big brown eyes. 'I also told her I'm not going ahead with my engagement. I'm going back to London on Saturday to talk to Julian.'

He studied her features for a moment's silence. 'I see.'

The tip of her tongue slipped out to moisten her lips. 'I think you're right,' she said. 'I need more time to think about my future.' She paused for a moment, her eyes still meshed with his. 'You were right about something else.' Another little pause. 'I'm not in love with him. I don't think I was ever in love with him.'

'What made you finally realise that?' Edoardo asked.

There was something in her eyes as she held his gaze that tugged on his heart like a small child pulling at his mother's skirt. 'I guess I must have finally grown up,' she said. 'Took me long enough, didn't it?'

He put her from him and stepped a couple of strides away, shoving a hand through his hair. 'I don't want you to get the wrong idea, Bella,' he said. 'I told you what I was prepared to offer. We can continue our affair, but that's all it will ever be.'

She looked at him with such raw longing that the tug on his heart became almost painful. 'We could have such a great future together,' she said.

'Your father trusted me to keep you safe,' Edoardo said. 'He didn't want you to throw your life away on an impulse. What you're doing now is exactly what he was worried about. Ten days ago you were determined to marry this Bellamy fellow, now you think you've suddenly developed feelings for me. Who's it going to be next week, or next month?'

'I haven't suddenly developed feelings for

you,' she said. 'These are not new feelings. I think they've been here all the time. I'm still getting my head around them. I need some time to think. These last few days have been amazing…but I'm not sure I can settle for an affair. I want the whole fairy tale.'

Edoardo let out a heavy sigh and brought her close again, resting his head on top of hers. 'I don't want to hurt you, Bella,' he said. 'But I just can't make those sorts of promises.' He breathed in the scent of her hair, felt her body melt against him like she was a part of him. He had never wanted anyone like he wanted her. He had thought his desire for her would have burned out by now but if anything it had become even more intense. He *ached* for her. But making a commitment to her, or to anyone, was beyond his capabilities. He could not envisage allowing someone—even someone as adorable and endearing as Bella—to have the power to abandon him.

He was the one who left when the time came.

He was the one who locked his feelings away so no one could exploit them.

He was the one who never loved.

Bella's infatuation with him would soon end. He was sure of it. She had fallen in and out of love ever since she'd hit her teens. Their little fling would run its course and she would go back to London and slot back into her high-society life.

At least this way she would never know how much he would miss her when she went.

Edoardo rose early the next morning. Not that he'd had a lot of sleep, but then neither had Bella, when it came to that. Making love with her during the night, knowing that she was leaving within the next twenty-four hours, had deeply unsettled him in spite of his resignation that things between them could go no further. He was used to distancing himself when relationships ran their course. He never suffered agonies of conscience or regret. He cut loose and moved on. Why, then, should it be any different this time? But something about the way Bella had curled up in his arms with her head resting against his chest had made something work loose inside his chest. Every time he took a breath, he felt it catch.

During the long hours before dawn, he had found himself dreaming of a future with her, of them living together at Haverton Manor as husband and wife. Of her happy laughter filling the empty rooms and halls of the house. He even thought of other laughter—the laughter of children, *their children*, running through the house, turning it into the home it was meant to be.

He tried to blink away the thoughts but they came back like moths circling around a light.

He could have it all.

He could have Bella *and* Haverton Manor.

They could build a family together, a solid, happy future.

She could leave him just like her mother had left Godfrey: devastated, alone, miserable.

The old panic seized him. How long before Bella wanted the bright lights of the city instead of his company? How long before her interest in him waned—a week? A month? A year? How could he live on that knife-edge? Every day would be an agony of wondering if it was going to be the last. He was used to disappointment. He had taught himself to always be prepared for it. It was easier to have nothing than to have everything and then lose it.

But then an even more disturbing thought joined the others. What if she didn't care for him at all? What if her little fling with him had been nothing more than payback all along? She had been vocal right from the start about her fury at him inheriting her childhood home. What better way to get back at him than pretend to be in love with him only to walk away so the press could pity or pillory him in equal measure?

He turned to his computer in an effort to distract himself, but as he pulled up the newspapers online, his eyes started to narrow in anger. It seemed he didn't have to wait in agonised anticipation for Bella's betrayal.

It was already there for everyone to see.

Bella came downstairs after sleeping in until ten in the morning. Edoardo had kept her awake for hours making passionate love with her. She could still feel the movement of his body in hers with each step she took. She wondered if he was feeling the wrench as she was about leaving for London the following day. Was that why there had been that edge of desperation in his love-making last night? He had held her for hours, his arms wrapped around her as if he never wanted to let her go. She had longed for him to say the words she most longed to hear, but he had said nothing. She was hoping her trip back to London would show him how much she had come to mean to him. Surely he would soon see how empty the days and nights were without her?

He was proud and private. It would take him a while to see what he was throwing away; it would take him even longer to admit to it. But after last night she felt a little glow of confidence burning inside her. It had *felt* like he loved her last night. He hadn't said the words out loud but his body had said them for him. All he needed was some time to come to terms with his feelings. He was used to locking them away. He was used to denying them. But how long could he deny the powerful connection they had forged? It wasn't just great sex. It was a connection that went far deeper than that. She felt close to him in a way she had never felt with anyone before. He had let her in to the most private part of his being. She *knew* him now. She knew his values, his strengths and weaknesses, his true self.

Bella pushed open the study door and found him standing stiffly in front of the window. 'Edoardo?' she said.

He turned and raked her from head to foot

with his gaze. It wasn't one of his smouldering 'I want to make love with you' looks. It was much more menacing than that. 'I've spoken with the lawyer,' he said in a cold, hard voice that was nothing like the deep, sexy rumble she had heard during the night and early hours of the morning.

'Pardon?'

He shoved a sheaf of papers towards her on the desk. 'You're on your own,' he said. 'I'm no longer your financial guardian.'

Bella swallowed and took an uncertain step towards the desk. 'What are you talking about? What do you mean? I don't understand...'

His eyes were like blue-green chips of ice. 'I want you out of here within the hour,' he said. 'Don't bother packing. I'll get Mrs Baker to do it when she comes back, plus everything else of yours left in the nursery. I want nothing of yours left in this house.'

'Edoardo... What are you say—?'

'It was a good plan.' His hands were tight fists

by his rigid sides. 'Very convincing, too. Not many people manage to pull the wool over my eyes but I have to hand it to you—you came pretty damn close.'

Bella felt a chill freeze her spine. 'What plan? I'm not following you. You're not making sense. Why are you being so beastly all of a sudden?'

He swung the computer screen around so she could see it. 'That's what you've done,' he said. 'You planned it from the start, didn't you? It was the perfect revenge. I can't believe how well you set me up.'

Bella looked at the computer screen where he had pulled up a selection of online newspapers. The headlines made her heart screech to a stop:

Self-Made Tycoon's Tragic Past Revealed
Former Bad Boy Victim of Child Abuse
Affair with Heiress Heals Wounded Heart-throb

There was a photograph of Edoardo kissing her in front of Haverton Manor. It had been taken only a couple of days ago—obviously through a telephoto lens, as Bella couldn't recall seeing anyone about. But then she remembered the journalists she had run into in the village. Had they been spying on them? Had they dug a little deeper in to his past? She looked up at him in bewilderment. 'You think *I* set this up?' she asked.

'Don't give me that doe-eyed, innocent look,' he said through tight lips. 'Get the hell out of here before I throw you out.'

'I didn't do this,' Bella said. 'How can you *think* I would do something like this? Don't you know me at all?'

His eyes flashed pure hatred at her. 'You were the *only* person who could have done it,' he said. 'I've told no one about my past. Not a damn soul. Now the whole bloody world knows about it, thanks to you. I knew I shouldn't have trusted you. You've always been a little two-faced cow. You wanted to get me back for not agreeing to your engagement. Well, you can marry whomever you like. I don't give a damn.'

Bella was reeling with shock, hurt and disbelief. 'I can't believe you think I would do this to you on purpose,' she said. 'There were journalists in the village when I went down for milk yesterday. I didn't tell you because—'

'Because you lured them down here with a tell-all exclusive, didn't you?' he said with a snarl. 'What did you think that last headline was going to do—force me to get down on bended knee and ask you to marry me?'

Bella glanced at the *Affair with Heiress Heals Wounded Heartthrob* headline. She swallowed tightly and looked at him again. 'I didn't say anything to them about...' She flushed and dropped her gaze. 'I might have mentioned something to my mother...'

He let out an expletive. 'So the two of you cooked this up, did you?' he said. 'I should've guessed. That's why she came down a couple of days ahead of you, to scope out the scene.'

'No,' Bella said, her heart sinking in despair. 'That's not what happened at all. I didn't do it on purpose. I just mentioned you'd had a terrible childhood. She was saying mean things about you and I thought—'

'You thought you'd have a cosy little gossip and destroy everything I've worked so hard for,' he said bitterly.

'Why does people knowing about your past destroy anything?' Bella asked. 'You've got nothing to be ashamed of. People will admire you for being so resilient. I know they will.'

His eyes glittered with contempt. 'I don't expect you to understand,' he bit out. 'You love all the attention. You're never out of the damn papers. You couldn't have picked a better way to get back at me. I value my privacy about everything. You *knew* that.' He curled his lip. 'All that talk of love and wanting the fairy tale—what a load of rubbish. You don't love anyone but yourself. You never have.'

Bella was struggling not to break down. Only

her pride kept her from having an emotional meltdown. She was so hurt, so devastated that he believed her to be capable of such loathsome behaviour. But it wasn't just his lack of trust that hurt her the most. He was pushing her away, locking her out, *rejecting* her. It was so crushing to be dismissed as if she had meant nothing to him other than a temporary diversion—a pretty toy that hadn't turned out to be all it had promised to be. If he cared even an iota for her, wouldn't he be doing everything to try to understand how this had come about? Wouldn't he understand that her openness was not wrong, just different from his need for privacy? 'I guess that's it, then,' she said, straightening her shoulders. 'I'll get on my way.'

'I never want to see you again,' he said as he glowered at her broodingly. 'Do you understand? Never.'

'Don't worry,' she said with a toss of her head as she swung away to the door. 'You won't.'

CHAPTER ELEVEN

IT WAS weeks before the furore in the press died down. Just about every person who had ever had anything to do with Edoardo during his childhood came out of the woodwork to give an exclusive. The worst of it was that even though his stepfather was now dead, his new wife and family sprang to his defence as if he had been a plaster saint. No doubt having been assured that no one could prosecute a dead man, they made him out to be the victim of a smear campaign.

It totally disgusted Bella. She felt sick every time she saw another article. She felt to blame, even though all she had tried to do was make her mother understand how difficult his childhood had been for Edoardo.

Her mother was unrepentant, however. Bella

had hoped Claudia might contact Edoardo and apologise, but her mother seemed to relish the fact that his tragic past was being talked about by every man and woman on the street.

Bella had thought about contacting him herself and explaining that it had been her mother who had given the tell-all interview to the press, but she knew he wouldn't believe her. He didn't trust her. He didn't trust anyone.

The lawyer had contacted Bella and she now had full control of her finances. But it was a bittersweet victory. She had more money than she knew what to do with.

But she felt terribly, achingly lonely.

The nights were the worst. Her friends would try to get her to go out with them to party or for dinner but she preferred to stay at home, curl up on the sofa and mindlessly watch whatever was on television. Sometimes she didn't even have the energy to switch it on; instead she would sit staring blankly into space, wondering how someone with so much wealth could be so miserably, desperately unhappy.

Julian had been gracious about her breaking off their relationship, which more or less confirmed that her decision to end it had been the right one. He had seemed more concerned that she would still donate a large sum to his mission. If he had truly loved her, wouldn't he have fought just a little bit for her?

Which brought her thoughts right back to Edoardo. He hadn't fought for her either. He hadn't even given her the benefit of the doubt. He had evicted her from his life as if she meant nothing to him.

Bella blew out a breath and tossed the sofa cushion to the floor. There was no point thinking about Edoardo. She was going to be on the other side of the world this time next week. She had organised a trip to Thailand to visit the orphanage she was now the proud patron of. So far she had managed to keep *that* out of the press. She couldn't wait to get away and put this whole dreadful episode behind her.

Edoardo was brooding over some plans for a big development he was working on in a nearby county when Mrs Baker came in with his coffee. He had a migraine starting at the backs of his eyes, the third one he'd had this week. It felt like dress-making pins were being drilled into each eyeball. 'Thanks,' he said, briefly glancing at her.

Mrs Baker stood with her arms folded across her ample chest, her lips pressed firmly together.

'Is there a problem?' he asked.

'Have you seen today's papers?'

He kept his gaze trained on the plans in front of him. 'I haven't looked at the paper in weeks,' he said. 'There's nothing of interest to me in them.'

Mrs Baker took a folded up paper out of her

apron pocket and handed it to him. 'I think you need to see this,' she said. 'It's about our Bella.'

Edoardo looked at the folded newspaper without touching it. 'Take it away,' he said and returned to his plans. 'I have no interest in what she's up to. It has nothing to do with me any more.'

Mrs Baker unfolded the paper and started to read. '"Society heiress Arabella Haverton has been named as the much-speculated about, anonymous patron for an orphanage in Thailand. Miss Haverton has reputedly already spent hundreds of thousands of pounds on food, clothing and toys for the children. She refused to confirm or deny the rumour when she boarded a flight to Bangkok yesterday."' She lowered the paper and gave Edoardo a beady look. 'Well, what do you think?'

He leaned back in his chair, rolling a pen between his finger and thumb. 'Good for her,' he said.

Mrs Baker frowned. 'Is that all you can say?'

He tossed the pen to the desk. 'What do you want me to say?' he asked. 'I don't care what she spends her money on. I told you—it's nothing to do with me any more.'

The housekeeper puffed herself up like a broody hen. 'What if something happens to her over there?' she asked. 'What if she gets some horrible tropical disease?'

He gave her a bored look before turning back to his papers. 'They do have doctors over there, you know.'

Mrs Baker's voice choked up. 'What if she decides to stay there?' she asked. 'What if she *never* comes back?'

Edoardo drew in a short breath and glowered at her. 'Why should that be of any concern to me?' he asked. 'I'm glad to see the back of her.' *Liar,* he thought. *You miss her so much, you're almost sick with it.*

'You're not,' Mrs Baker said, speaking his thoughts out loud. 'You're miserable. You're like a bear with a sore head. You're not the same man since she was down here with you. Even Fergus is off his food.'

Edoardo picked up his pen again and started clicking it for something to do with his hands. He wasn't sure he liked being *that* transparent. Next thing, he would be made a fool of in the press for being heartbroken over his failed relationship with Bella. That would be the last straw. He was not going to be painted as a lovesick fool, not if he could help it. 'That's because Fergus is old,' he said.

'Yes, well, one day you'll be old too,' Mrs Baker said. 'And what will you have to show for your life? A fancy house and more money than you can poke a stick at, but no one to mop your brow when you have one of your headaches, no one to smile at you and tell you they love you more than life itself. A blind man could see Bella isn't capable of spilling her guts to the press. She's open with people, but that's what's so loveable about her. She wears her heart on her sleeve. No, that leak to the press was the work of her mother.' She slapped the paper on his desk. 'You can read all about Claudia Alvarez's exclusive interview on her daughter's charity efforts on page twenty.'

Edoardo frowned as he looked at the paper lying on his desk. He had already considered the possibility that Bella wasn't responsible for that leak to the press. He knew what journalists were like. And, yes, Mrs Baker was right; Bella was like an open book when it came to her feelings.

But it didn't change a thing.

He didn't want to expose himself to the pain of loving someone, especially someone like Bella. She was flighty and impulsive. How long would it be before she fell in love with someone else? He would feel abandoned all over again. He couldn't bear to feel that wretched feeling of having no one—no one at all.

He was fine on his own. He was used to it.

He would get used to it again.

Sure, it had been miserably lonely around

here without her. The house seemed too big for him now; the empty rooms mocked him as he wandered past. His bedroom was the worst. He could barely stand to be in there with the lingering trace of Bella's perfume haunting him. The long, wide corridors echoed with his solitary footsteps. It even felt colder in spite of him cranking up the heating. Even Fergus kept looking up at him with a hangdog look on his face, reminding him that all the colour and joy had gone out of his life. *He* had sent it out of his life. He had sent Bella away when the one thing he wanted was to have her close.

He raised his gaze back to the housekeeper's. 'Don't you have work to do?' he asked.

Mrs Baker pursed her lips. 'That girl loves you,' she said. 'And you love her but you're too darned stubborn to tell her. You're even too stubborn to admit it to yourself.'

'Will that be all?' he asked with an arched brow.

'She's probably crying herself to sleep every

night,' she said. 'Her father would be spin-ning in his grave; I'm sure of it. He thought you would do the right thing by her. But you've abandoned her when she needed you the most.'

He pushed back his chair and got to his feet. 'I don't want to listen to this.' *I know I've been a stupid fool. I don't need my housekeeper to tell me. I need time to think how I'm going to dig my way out of this and win Bella back. Is there a way to win her back? Isn't it already too late?*

Mrs Baker's eyes watered up. 'This is her home,' she said. 'She belongs here.'

'I know,' he said as he expelled a long, uneven breath. 'That's why I'm sending her the deeds. The lawyers are sorting it out as we speak.'

Mrs Baker's eyes rounded. 'You're not going to live here any more?'

'No.' Giving up Haverton Manor was the easy bit. Losing Bella was the thing that gutted him the most. What had he been thinking? *Had* he been thinking? What would the rest of his life be like if she went off and married someone else? What if she had *their* children instead of his? How could he bear it? He wanted her. He *loved* her. He adored her. She was his world, his future, his *heart*. But it was too late. He had hurt her terribly. She would never forgive him now. He didn't dare hope she would. He was already preparing himself for the disappointment. It was best if he took himself out of the picture and let her get on with her life. He had never belonged in it in the first place.

'But what about Fergus?' Mrs Baker asked.

'Bella can look after him,' he said. 'He's her father's dog, after all.'

'But that old dog loves you,' she said. 'How can you just walk away?'

He gave her a grim look. 'It's for the best.'

Bella spent the first few days at the orphanage in a state of deep culture-shock. She barely ate or slept. It wasn't that the children weren't being cared for properly, more that she couldn't quite get her head or her heart around the fact that the little babies and children she played with daily had nobody in their lives other than the orphanage workers. She spent most nights sobbing herself to sleep at their heartbreaking plight. Each day from dawn till late at night she gathered them close and tried to give them all the love and joy they had missed out on. She showered them with affection and praise. She played with them and read to them; she even sang to them with the few nursery rhymes she remembered from her own early childhood before her mother had left.

'You will exhaust yourself if you don't take a proper break now and again,' Tasanee, one of the senior workers, said during Bella's second week.

Bella kissed the top of an eight-week-old baby girl's downy head as she cradled her close against her chest. 'I don't want to put Lawan down until she goes to sleep,' she said. 'She cries unless someone is holding her. She must be missing her mother. She must sense she's never coming back.' *And I know what it's like to feel so alone and abandoned.*

'It is sad that her mother and father died,' Tasanee said as she touched the baby's cheek with her finger. 'But we have a couple lined up to adopt her. The paperwork is being processed. She will have a good life. It is easier for the babies; they don't remember their real parents. It's the older ones who have the most trouble adjusting.'

Bella looked across to where a group of children were playing. There was a little boy of about five who was standing on the outside of the group. He didn't join in the noisy game. He didn't interact with anyone. He just stood there watching everything with a serious look on his face. He reminded her of Edoardo. How frightening it must have been for him to feel so alone, to face daily the horrible abuse from a vindictive stepfather. Bella ached for the little boy he had once been. She ached for the future she so desperately wanted with him but now could never have. She determined she would do all she could for each and every one of these children so that they would not suffer what he had suffered.

'Miss Haverton?' Sumalee, another one of the orphanage helpers, came across to Bella once she had put Lawan down for her nap. 'This came for you in the post.'

Bella took the A4 envelope. 'Thanks.' She peeled it open and took out the document inside. Her eyes nearly popped out of her head when she saw what it was. 'I think there's been a mistake…'

'What's wrong?' Sumalee asked.

Bella gnawed at her lip as she shuffled through the other papers that had come with the deeds to Haverton Manor. 'I think I might have to go back to Britain to sort this out…'

'Will you come back soon?' Sumalee said.

Bella tucked the document back inside the envelope and gave the young girl a quick, reassuring smile. 'Don't worry. I'll be back as soon as I can,' she said. 'I have to see a man about a dog.'

Edoardo was loading the last of his things in his car when he saw a sports car come speeding up the driveway. Fergus got up from the front step and started wagging his tail, a soft whine sounding from his throat. 'For God's sake, don't gush,' Edoardo said out of the side of his mouth. 'She's probably only back to argue over some of the fine print.'

Bella got out of the car and came towards him, bringing the scent of spring flowers with her. 'What the hell is going on?' she asked, waving a sheet of paper at him.

'It's yours,' Edoardo said. 'The manor is yours, and so is Fergus.'

Her brows jammed together over her nose. 'Are you without *any* feeling at all?' she asked. 'That dog loves you. How can you just—' she waved her hands about theatrically '—just hand him over like a parcel you don't want?'

'I can't take him with me.'

'Why not?' she asked. 'Where are you going?'

'Away.'

'Away where?'

He slammed the boot. 'I don't belong here. It's your home, not mine.'

She shoved the papers at him. 'I don't want it.'

He shoved the papers back. 'I don't want it either,' he said.

She glowered at him. 'Why are you doing this?'

'Your father was wrong to give me your home,' he said. 'This is your last connection with him. I don't feel right about taking it from you.'

'It's your last connection with him too,' she said.

He gave a shrug. 'Yes, well, I have plenty of memories that will make up for that.'

'You can't just walk away,' Bella said. 'What about Fergus? I thought you loved him.'

Edoardo bent down and ruffled the old dog's

ears. 'I do love him,' he said. 'He's been an amazing friend.' He straightened. 'But it's time I moved on.'

'So you're just going to leave?' she asked.

'It's for the best, Bella,' he said.

'The best for whom?' she asked. 'Fergus is going to pine for you; you know he will. And what about Mrs Baker? She's devoted her life to looking after you. Are you just going to walk away from everyone who loves you?'

He opened the driver's door of his car. 'Goodbye, Bella.'

Bella put her hands on her hips. 'You're not going to say it, are you?' she said. 'You're too proud or too stubborn or both to admit that you care for someone. That you *need* someone, that you actually *love* someone.'

His eyes met hers. 'Will telling you I love you erase the horrible things I said to you?' he asked.

She gave a huffy lift of one shoulder, her expression still cross. 'I don't know… It wouldn't hurt to try.'

Edoardo felt a corner of his mouth lift up. How cute was she, with that haughty look on her face? She was trying to be angry but he could see the love shining through the cracks of her armour. It gave him hope. It eased the painful ache of impending disappointment he always carried with him. 'Will telling you I love you make you forgive me for sending you away like that?' he asked.

She gave another little shrug, but this time a tiny sparkle came into her eyes. 'I don't mind a bit of grovelling when it's warranted,' she said.

Edoardo looked into her toffee-brown eyes and felt a giant wave of emotion roll through him. How could he not love her? Hadn't he *always* loved her? When had he *not* loved her? 'I guess I'd better get started, then,' he said. 'This could take a while. You're not in a hurry, are you?'

Her eyes glinted some more. 'I'll make the time,' she said. 'I wouldn't want to miss this for the world.'

He took a breath as he captured both of her hands in his. 'I'm sorry for what I said, for how I treated you, for how I pushed you away.' He pulled her into his chest, burying his head against the side of her neck. 'I'm not the right person for you. I don't know how to love someone without holding back.'

'Yes, you do,' she said, pulling back to look up at him with adoring eyes. 'You do know how to love. I've seen it in so many ways. You're exactly like my father. You don't say it with words. You say it in actions.'

He stroked her face as if he couldn't quite believe she was here in person. 'I've missed you so much,' he said. 'I can't believe I sent you away like that. It was cruel and heartless. But if it's any consolation, I hurt myself just as much. Maybe that's why I did it. On some deeply subconscious level, I didn't feel I deserved to be loved by you.'

'I didn't betray you to the press,' she said with a solemn look. 'Not intentionally, at least. I just didn't like the way everyone was making you out to be the one at fault. It made me so angry. I wanted to put them straight.'

'I know you didn't do it on purpose,' he said. 'I think I knew that from the start. I was just looking for an excuse to send you away. You got too close. I wasn't able to handle it. I've spent most of my life pushing people away—even people who cared about me.'

Bella nestled closer. 'I love you,' she said. 'I love everything about you. I think I probably always have.'

He put her from him so he could meet her gaze. 'I think your father knew that,' he said. 'He was so afraid you would rush off and marry the first man who asked you. He made me promise to keep you from marrying any-one before you were twenty-five. But it looks like I'm going to have to break my promise to him after all.'

She looked at him quizzically. 'What do you mean?'

'Will you marry me?' he asked.

Bella gaped at him. 'But I thought you never wanted to...?'

'That was before,' he said. 'I've seen the error of my ways. Besides, what am I going to say to Mrs Baker? She's going to have my guts for garters if I don't do the right thing by you.'

Bella looped her arms around his neck and smiled at him. 'We can't have Mrs Baker upset, now, can we?'

He grinned at her. 'So, is that a yes?'

Her eyes were brimming with happy tears as she looked up at him. 'When have I ever been able to say no to you?'

He cupped her face in his hands and locked his gaze on hers. 'I love you. I've never said that to anyone before, but I plan to say it every day for the rest of our lives.'

She smiled up at him radiantly. 'I love you too.'

'I want to have a baby with you,' he said, rubbing his nose against hers. 'Maybe even two babies. And then maybe we can adopt a couple of children.'

'I want that too,' she said, letting out a little sigh of bliss. 'I want it so much.'

'Then we'd better get started, don't you think?' he said.

'What?' she said, pretending to be shocked. 'Right now?'

'Right now,' he said and scooped her up in his arms and carried her towards the house.

* * * * *

Mills & Boon® Large Print
June 2013

SOLD TO THE ENEMY
Sarah Morgan

UNCOVERING THE SILVERI SECRET
Melanie Milburne

BARTERING HER INNOCENCE
Trish Morey

DEALING HER FINAL CARD
Jennie Lucas

IN THE HEAT OF THE SPOTLIGHT
Kate Hewitt

NO MORE SWEET SURRENDER
Caitlin Crews

PRIDE AFTER HER FALL
Lucy Ellis

ER ROCKY MOUNTAIN PROTECTOR
Patricia Thayer

THE BILLIONAIRE'S BABY SOS
Susan Meier

BABY OUT OF THE BLUE
Rebecca Winters

ALLROOM TO BRIDE AND GROOM
Kate Hardy